CONSCIOUS

Book Three in the Influence Series

By David R. Bernstein

Copyright © 2020 by David R. Bernstein. All rights reserved.

TORMENT PUBLISHING

No part of this publication may be reproduced, stored in a retrieval system, or transmitted in any form or by any means, electronic, mechanical, photocopying, recording, or otherwise, without written permission of the author.

This is a work of fiction. Names, characters, places, and incidents are either the product of the author's imagination or are used fictitiously. Any resemblance to actual persons, living or dead, are purely coincidental.

Bernstein, David R.
Conscious

ISBN: 979-8600914247

For more information on reproducing sections of this book or sales of this book, go to www.davidrbernstein.com or www.tormentpublishing.com

10 9 8 7 6 5 4 3 2 1

Contents:

CHAPTER ONE 5
CHAPTER TWO 15
CHAPTER THREE 27
CHAPTER FOUR 34
CHAPTER FIVE 43
CHAPTER SIX 54
CHAPTER SEVEN 70
CHAPTER EIGHT 82
CHAPTER NINE 92
CHAPTER TEN 101
CHAPTER ELEVEN 109
CHAPTER TWELVE 125
CHAPTER THIRTEEN 132
CHAPTER FOURTEEN 141
CHAPTER FIFTEEN 151
CHAPTER SIXTEEN 162
CHAPTER SEVENTEEN 172
CHAPTER EIGHTEEN 177
CHAPTER NINETEEN 185

CHAPTER ONE

THREE BODIES HANG from the overpass, nooses cutting deep into their necks. There's a grease-stained sheet draped over the railing just above their bodies with the words 'We Own Our Minds' spray-painted in red.

I try to muster up an appropriate emotional response to the grisly scene, but nothing comes. At this point, I'm just numb. This is the third such message we've received in the last couple of weeks since fleeing Seattle—what was left of it anyway. The first was waiting for us at the Protectors' former base, graffitied onto a car in the alley just outside the abandoned research facility. Smoke billowed from the blown-off door, and those of us who braved the fire to search for survivors found only the charred and crumbling remains of several Protectors who had been strapped into metal chairs to be burned alive. We've been on the run ever since.

But the messages aren't just for the Protectors. Reports keep pouring in from all over that Influencers are being cornered and tortured like wild dogs before finally being slaughtered or, more often it seems, left to die slowly and alone. The overwhelming cruelty of it all has switched off my feelings. Most Influencers are not like Jax, Stratton, Ava, or me. They're not able to defend themselves with their abilities. They're simple mood-adjusters. If I let myself feel the rage this injustice deserves, I think I would explode in a ball of flames.

"Let's keep moving," Leeyah orders. "We need to try to get out of the city before nightfall. Keep your awareness extended."

We have no choice but to pass directly under the dangling corpses. The stench forces our noses into shirt collars and elbow crooks. Flies drop down, buzzing around our exposed eyes as if checking to see if we might taste better alive. I remember something I heard a long time ago when me and my sister Amanda were still stuck in the Lost Soul shelter as kids: flies puke every time they land. The thought of what these flies might be throwing up on us, however tiny the amounts, makes me clamp my shirt collar extra tight over my mouth. I swallow the bile and the feelings that might have bubbled up with it.

"Okay over there?" Farren asks from the muffled cover of his arm.

"Sure, why wouldn't I be?" I choke out.

Our eyes meet over our makeshift hazard masks and nothing more needs to be said.

As our group emerges into the dismal sunlight on the other side of the overpass, there is a collective scuffle and sigh as we drop our coverings and breathe in the somewhat fresher air over here. The road ahead of us is just as buckled and blackened from bombings as the road behind us, and the cross streets cutting between the buildings lining it could be hiding legions of people who want us all dead. The Southern Alliance and the sectors that joined up with them have been paying Harvester clans to hunt Influencers down. Money is useless now, of course, but food and supplies are extremely motivating. Not to mention that Harvesters have always lived for this type of chaos.

But my extended awareness tells me the immediate coast is clear. Perhaps the chaos has become too much for even the desperate Harvesters to stand. What little order the sector groups were previously able to enforce has vanished. Without the manipulated Influencers those sectors were using to control their citizens, all that remains in their cities is fear and violence.

As we make our way into the heart of whatever city this is, or used to be, I turn back to see Jax trailing behind our group, head down. His parents, my aunt and uncle, may not have intended for this to be the outcome of their actions, but they certainly did their part in bringing on this new world. Jax hasn't been the same since we left Seattle. He barely talks anymore, and the leader everyone once knew has vanished as completely as the people of this city. Seeing him so broken is just about the only thing that puts a crack in this wall around my heart.

Farren's arm brushes mine, pulling my attention away from Jax. I loop my elbow through his and lean my head on his shoulder as we walk.

"He just needs more time," Farren murmurs into my hair. "Everything that happened was… a lot."

"I know that," I snap. "It was a lot for me too, but…" I trail off before I say something I'll immediately feel guilty for. It wouldn't be true anyway. I'm just better at looking like I'm doing better than he is, I guess.

Farren nods—though I'm not really sure what he's agreeing with—and kisses my forehead. The rest of the group has passed us by while we were hanging all over each other, so we ease apart and hurry to catch up.

Leeyah remains in the lead with Stratton trailing behind her. The last few weeks he's become closer with her. I guess he needs some sort of mother figure in his life, but I'm not really liking the idea of it being *my* mother.

"Can you believe that?" I mutter to Farren, trying not to glower too openly at Stratton. "If he starts calling her mom before I even start calling her that, I'm going to leave *him* on an overpass."

Farren chuckles dutifully, but I can tell my 'joke' made him uncomfortable. "You can forgive him for everything else he did to us, but not that?"

"He didn't have much choice about all that, but this…"

Farren slides his arm around my shoulders. "Well, you could have it all wrong, you know. He might just have a crush on her. She's pretty fine for a woman her—"

"Gross!" I pull away from him and jab my elbow into his side. "Shut up!"

Farren feigns a grimace and then smirks. "I'm just saying…"

"What?" I glare at him. "Do *you* have a crush on my mom?"

He glances up at her with an appraising squint and then shrugs. I give him another jab before he can say anything that makes me have to break up with him. Although I'm not sure even that would do it. Farren's one of the few bright spots in life right now. No matter how empty I start to feel, he finds some way to make me smile again. Somewhere between Seattle and whatever hell hole we've stumbled into today, we became a real couple, not just a way to pass the time between taking down sector groups.

"You are such an idiot," Amanda blurts from behind me.

Thinking she's talking to me, I crane my neck to glare at her. But her eyes are on Caiden; she's not paying any attention to me at all. That's taken some time getting used to, but it's honestly a relief not to bear the brunt of her nurturing tendency any longer. Caiden might be older than her—too old for their verbally sparring friendship to take a romantic turn, I believe—but he could use someone looking out for him emotionally when he's getting too worked up about war things.

I turn my attention forward again. Not far behind Leeyah, Ava and Envee walk hand-in-hand. Since Seattle, Ava has, more than ever, taken Envee under her wing. That's another source of relief. At only eleven years old, Envee needs someone mature to care for her, and honestly, I think Ava needs her just as much since losing Maddux. They're good for each other.

But as we continue easing our way into the destroyed city, I'm wondering if this plan is really good for any of us. Our numbers have dwindled considerably since fleeing Seattle. We had to let all of the captured Vernon Society fighters go—even Captain Relic. There were just too many prisoners for us to manage while also keeping ourselves alive. Not with the Southern Alliance and all their news pals trying to hunt us down.

The only prisoner we kept is Miya. None of the Protectors are really happy about that, but she wanted nothing to do with the other Society members. Forcing her to go it alone seemed too cruel. Nance keeps a close eye on Miya, and so far, we haven't had to regret letting her stick around. She's even given us some good intel on the surrounding sector groups, so I'm not too worried about her stabbing us in the back. On that front, I'm way more concerned about Captain Relic showing up again when we least expect it.

Farren slips his hand down my forearm and interlocks his fingers with mine. "Your mom is relentless. Don't get me wrong, I want to keep you out of harm's way just as much as she does, but we have to think about our next step and not just keep moving from area to area like this. It's not accomplishing... anything."

I look up to meet his eyes. "She just got me back, and at the expense of losing her sister and most of her people. I think she just wants to keep me alive however possible."

Farren's about to say something when my pulsing heartbeat thuds behind my ears, triggering me to awaken my consciousness. Something has changed.

"We've got movement up ahead," Leeyah says, stopping at an intersection. "Let's duck into this bus station and open our awareness."

Our group moves in closer together, funneling inside a busted-up entry that leads into a hollowed-out passenger station. Broken glass is spread all over the floor, and tattered furniture is strewn about. Leeyah waits until everyone is safely inside, before shutting the door and locking it. Caiden instructs people to take cover behind the station's counters and desks.

Leeyah—my *mom*, I mentally correct—hasn't been able to use her full Push abilities in ages, but miraculously for us, she can still sense people nearby. She's not sure why that is, and the rest of us sure don't know. Push abilities always fade with age. Ava is only twenty-seven and she's the oldest person who can still Push that any of us have ever met.

Farren guides me to a toppled over table and we crouch down together, huddling in close. Peering over the top of the cracked table, I watch Jax and the others safely hide away. There's no need for Leeyah or Caiden to bark further instructions at us, we all know what to do in these situations—keep quiet and push out our awareness.

My breathing slows as I focus on the greater surroundings. Pops of pure energy drift in and out of my mind. The ability to Push animals sometimes makes surveilling an area difficult. I swipe through the simple life forms in my mind and reach farther until I pick up on a smallish group of people a few streets over. Sensing people this far away always reminds me of the feeling that someone is looking over your shoulders when no one is actually there.

I meet Leeyah's gaze, and her eyes widen, fully understanding that I've detected something. "Ten to fifteen people, two or three blocks away," I whisper, just loud enough for her to hear me. Something about talking softly, even when we don't really have to, makes me feel more comfortable.

Turning to face the back of the station, I look to Jax who leans up against the far counter. He's always been able to sense the intentions of people better than I have. He simply shakes his head and I know what that means. These people are not our friends.

"We should wait them out," Nance says to Leeyah. "That's a pretty big group to deal with."

"We need to get a better look at them," Caiden says, eyeing me. "If they're just Harvesters, we will take them out, but if they're an organized search party from a sector group, we should probably avoid them. Our ammo is running low."

"Caiden's right," Leeyah says. "If they're from a sector group, they'll be able to outgun us."

Over the last few days, we've been actively taking out Harvester hunting packs that have been looking for roaming Influencers. It's been fairly easy since they don't have the block implants that keep us out of their heads, but sector groups are different. They're usually very well prepared in both their offense and defense. We've got to get a better look at what we're up against here. "I'll get eyes on them," I say to Leeyah.

She gives me an encouraging nod. She knows my Push abilities have never been stronger. Ever since the traumatic end to the Vernon Society, it's like a switch inside of me has been flipped. Leeyah believes every Influencer has a breaking point where their ability becomes one with their mind. Watching my aunt and uncle be incinerated by bombs from above must have been my trigger.

I take a deep breath and go inside my thoughts. My surroundings fall silent, and I'm able to expand my awareness within a few moments. Bright pinpricks of light dot my inner field of vision. As I search the sky and the tops of the surrounding buildings, an eagle's pure essence comes into focus. Perched on the top of a tall tower, I unfold my awareness into the bird and take it over. The sky is now mine.

A wash of calmness circles my awareness as I fly with the bird into the cool air above. Hazy fog blankets the tops of the buildings, so I dip lower toward the oncoming group.

One hundred yards below, the group emerges from the gloom. They are splintered into several packs as they move through the crumbling urban landscape, heading directly toward our position, but I still can't tell who they are. A rusted traffic light dangles above the intersection they are fast approaching. My wings extend as I glide down and latch onto the wire connecting the light.

My own alarm ruffles the birds' wings. The group is larger than I felt. There are at least twenty or twenty-five of them, all heavily armed with assault rifles. They are definitely not Harvesters.

I'm about to pull my awareness back when I spot a man staring right at me. My Push flutters between the bird and my body at the bus station. It can't be. But it is.

Scars run up and down his face, but I know exactly who this is. He's older now, but I could never forget that face.

The man, dressed in full riot gear, cocks his head to the side and glares at me before pulling out his pistol. He scoffs, pulls the trigger, and everything goes black. As if someone grabbed my soul from behind, I'm yanked back into my body.

My eyes fly open and search the worried faces peeking over counters and furniture until they lock on Amanda. "It's Billy Wilson and he's out for blood."

CHAPTER TWO

"WHO THE HELL is Billy Wilson?" Caiden blurts out.

Amanda jabs him in the side with her elbow. "Keep it down, Idiot."

"Oww, what?" he whisper-whines, rubbing his side. "Am I supposed to know this?"

Amanda shakes her head and hisses, "He's someone we grew up with back at Lost Souls."

Caiden's mouth forms an understanding O. So she's told him this story before. Good. I didn't really want to get into it right now. Just thinking about that day rattles me enough, and I'm going to need all my wits about me for whatever lies ahead.

Leeyah carefully makes her way over to me, crouching to stay below the window line. She leans against the busted-up counter next to Farren and me. "Is he one of those bullies you told me about? That forced you to use your ability and—"

"Yes," I say, a little too sharply. "That's the one."

Leeyah's eyes soften in a way that lets me know she's filling up with guilt for not being around to raise me herself. I know that wasn't her fault, but it's easy in this moment to want to blame her anyway. My eyes seek out Amanda's. She's the one good thing to come of my time at Lost Souls, and the only other person here who can really understand how bad Billy Wilson's presence might be.

Amanda chews on her lip, eyes round with concern and yeah, fear. "I wasn't even sure if they survived. We left so fast…"

Farren places his warm hand on my shoulder. "How do you know it's him? That was a while back, Kaylin."

I swallow hard, suppressing a shudder. "I'd never forget that face. I can still see the same old hate and anger in his eyes."

"Did you say Billy Wilson?" Miya asks from across the room where she's crouching below the windows.

"What do you know?" Amanda demands, slipping back into mama bear mode.

Miya purses her lips as if debating how much to reveal. "Maybe I'm wrong. It's probably a fairly common name, after all."

"Miya," Farren barks. "Tell us what you know about *any* Billy Wilson."

Miya lifts her head over the dusty row of seats and peers out the window before facing us again. "A Commander William Wilson has been one of the top leaders in the Southern Alliance military for a couple of years now. He was always pushing us… I mean, the

Vernon Society... hard to hand over all of its Influencers." Miya eyes me suspiciously. "He seemed to have an unusually personal thirst for their blood."

A coolness washes over me, settling in my chest. "That sounds like Billy. What about his brother? What about Alex Wilson?"

Miya narrows her eyes as she ponders my question and then finally shakes her head. "I'm sorry, but I've never heard of an Alex Wilson before."

Amanda and I lock eyes, each of us seeing the memory of that day reflected there. The Wilson brothers' bodies crumpled on the cafeteria floor among dozens of cracked food trays, neither of them moving and both of them covered in blood.

"Kaylin?" Leeyah asks gently, glancing between us. "What are you two thinking?"

"Billy and Alex were practically conjoined," I tell my mother as a powerful fear creeps into my body, forcing me to shake so hard I can barely speak. "If Alex hasn't been heard from..."

"If he died that day, and Billy knows Kay is who he's after here, or recognizes her when he finds us, then we're all in big trouble," Amanda finishes for me.

Farren immediately wraps his arms around my waist and pulls me in close. "I won't let anything happen to you."

"Yes, Kaylin, your family will protect you," Leeyah adds, squeezing my hand. "Always."

I accept her comforting words but looking around at the faces of everyone who's made it this far, the truth is that whether or not I'll be able to protect my family is what's worrying me.

"Time's up," Jax says quietly from the back of the room. "They're almost here, and they all have the block implant. What's the plan?"

It used to be Jax's job to make the plan, but he relinquished that role weeks ago. Now, he looks to Leeyah to make the call. Her jaw twitches rapidly as she considers our options.

Caiden pulls his pistol from its holster with an impatient sigh. "Fight or flight, gang?"

I rise to one knee and lean on the counter. "Before Billy killed my host bird, I counted at least twenty-five of them—all heavily armed. I think we need to create a little bit of distance and re-evaluate this."

"Agreed," Leeyah says and then sets her sights on Jax. "We've got to move. Jax, lead the way and keep them on the outside your reach." Leeyah turns to Envee. "Amplify him, okay, hun?"

Without hesitation, Envee jumps to her feet, glances at Ava, and then makes her way toward Jax, whose face looks a little pale over having to take charge. Her nearly white-blond hair sways with her quick movements. Ava's jaw tightens, clearly not wanting the younger girl out of her sight, but she keeps her protest to herself. We all have jobs to do. Amplifying our Pushes is Envee's.

Everyone else springs into action. We've set up protocols for this sort of issue. Jax, with Envee holding his hand, navigates a seemingly senseless path through narrow alleys and empty side streets, with the sole goal of putting as much distance as we can between our team and Billy Wilson's. Who knows where will come out at. Miya, Amanda, and the remaining Protectors follow closely behind Jax and Envee. With weapons drawn, Caiden and Farren trail them with their sights open, scanning the surroundings for signs of trouble. Leeyah, Stratton, Ava, and I bring up the rear, expanding our awareness to protect the group as a whole.

It doesn't take long before Jax gives us the signal that he doesn't sense them anymore. As we huddle up to plan our next move, I pat my cousin on the shoulder and tell him he did a great job. He offers me the faintest of smiles in return. The first in a long while.

***

A cool breeze comes from the west as the sun dips below the horizon. There's been no sign of Billy Wilson's army for the last couple of hours. We've made camp at a dilapidated rest stop on the outskirts of the last city we traveled through. Luckily, there's still running water in the bathroom. I've always been amazed at how the utilities still work in some places. There might not be hot water, but at least we can clean up and regroup.

There's also a variety of vehicles abandoned in the parking lot. A few busted windows later and everyone has a soft bed to sleep on for a change. Farren somehow claims a whole RV for our private use, and since we're the only couple left in the group, no one argues.

Farren stands in front of the camper, arms extended and a smirk stretching across his face. "Our humble abode."

"It's nice, but does it have room service?" I chuckle. "You know how the Vernon Society spoiled me."

Farren drops his hands to his sides, feigning exasperation. "No, but... it does come with this guy." He points both thumbs at himself and waggles his eyebrows.

"Eh. No thanks." I shrug, biting down on my cheeks to keep from smiling. "I was really hoping for snacks. Chocolate? Fresh fruit? Anything?"

"Well, if you'll take *anything*," Farren says with a wink. "Then I can probably rustle you up some chips from the store. If you don't mind eating after mice, of course."

I make a face, although the truth is, I'd better get used to the idea. Our supplies can't last forever on the road like this.

"But seriously, I'll go scope it out," Farren offers, touching the small of my back in a way that makes me shiver. "You don't have to do that," I say, grabbing his hand. "I was joking."

He rolls his eyes. "I know, Kay, but it's a good idea anyway. We should never pass up a chance to scavenge non-perishables."

Laughing, I place a hand over my heart. "I bet you use that line on all the girls."

"Only the finest ladies, miss." He opens the camper door with a silly flourish. "Your private quarters await."

I step up into the RV, and for all our teasing, I might actually cry over the simple luxury of these accommodations. Farren's small electric lantern hums on the tiny kitchenette table, illuminating the equally tiny fridge, stove, and sink set into the counter on the opposite wall. A plush, plaid couch is wedged between the dining area and the driver's seat. A well-worn ballcap rests on the dashboard, faded from weeks in the sun. I wonder if its owner is missing it, or if he's even still alive. Probably not, if I'm honest with myself.

Turning from the eerie reminder of the human toll of this war, I discover a compact bedroom on the other side of the dining area. A large bed takes up most of the space, its floral-print comforter tucked in so neatly around the edges it may have never even been used. Two narrow cabinets frame the curtained window above the bed, and I suspect if I open them, I'll find clothes to go with the ballcap. How would these people feel about an Influencer occupying their space? Would they be sympathetic to our plight, or would their eyes fill up with fear and hate?

I'm pulled from my thoughts as a rattle comes from the entry. Amanda cranes her head through the opening. "Dude, nice setup." Her eyes pan over the camper as she steps all the way in. "I'm bunking up with Ava and Envee in an old minivan a few spots over."

"That sounds crowded. Do you want—"

"To listen to you lovebirds coo at each other back there all night?" She gives him an *oh, please* look.

A blush flares across my face, and I yank the bedroom door shut. "Shut up."

Amanda grins and punches me playfully on the arm. "I'll be fine in the minivan. You two enjoy a little privacy for a change. You deserve it today."

"I guess," I say, giving her a weird look. What does she mean? Because of Billy?

Amanda's grin only widens. Suddenly, she's pulling me into her arms and squeezing me until I think my ribs will crack. "I love you, Kay."

A warmth radiates in my chest, but it could just be my lungs collapsing from the force of her hug. "I love you too."

A few minutes after that sudden burst of affection, Amanda excuses herself and heads back to her van, claiming she's too tired to sit up another minute. I'm right there with her. Yawning—and wondering what's taking Farren so long—I make my way back the bedroom and stretch out on the bed. It's a pretty wild feeling after all this time on the run. I close my eyes, planning to sneak in a little cat nap before that slowpoke gets back.

But my mind won't shut off. All I see is Billy's angry face glaring at the eagle right before he pulled the trigger. *Did he know it was me?* The thought is ridiculous, I know. For Billy, killing harmless animals for no good reason is probably something he does every day But still, it felt so personal. Perhaps that was just a side effect from my mind merging with the bird's. I shudder, remembering the way it felt when my awareness snapped back into my own body at the instant of the eagle's death. I've never felt anything like that before. It was a sad lesson in being more careful with my hosts' lives. And my own. What if I hadn't snapped back?

The door squeaks open, interrupting my morbid thoughts. Farren pauses near the couch, looking around. I wiggle my foot to get his attention, and he grins as he thuds over to stand in the doorway. Farren reaches into his pocket and quickly yanks out a small brown wrapper that crinkles with every movement of his hand.

"You wanted chocolate? You got chocolate"

The stress of the day washes away as I scoot up to the edge of the bed and reach out for the treat. "No way. Where did you find that?"

He pulls it back and holds it up high, out of my reach. "Whoa there, not so fast. This is very special candy for a very special day."

I plant my arms behind me on the bed and look up at him. "What are you talking about?"

"You only turn eighteen once in your life," he says, his grin returning.

My head jerks back slightly, and I tilt my chin up and narrow my eyes on him. "Wait, what? How did you... I mean... is it really?"

I stopped tracking time ages ago. What good is it when every single day is the same? Walking and hiding and hunkering down. Wake up and repeat. I assumed everyone else had done the same. The fact that Farren not only knows what date it is, but that date is my birthday is... mind-blowing.

Farren's smile widens. "Well, your mom would probably know, wouldn't she?"

"Why didn't she say anything to me?" I say, furrowing my brow.

Farren laughs and ruffles my hair. "Because I begged her to let me say something first. It wasn't easy. If it were up to her and Amanda, we'd all be playing pin the tail on the donkey and pretending protein bars are cake." He shrugs, looking suddenly embarrassed. "I wanted a little alone time with you."

I grab his hand and yank him down beside me on the foot of the bed. "Not until you hand over the goods, mister."

Farren wraps one arm around my shoulders and sets the chocolate bar on my knee. There's a thin layer of dust on the wrapper, smudge by his fingerprints. I don't care. I rip the packaging off and start ravenously shoving the candy into my mouth. From the texture, it's clearly melted in some heat and then returned to a solid form at some point, maybe a few times actually, but the taste is divine all the same.

When it's all gone, and I'm licking my fingers like a toddler, Farren starts laughing.

"What did you think was going to happen?" I ask.

He shrugs, still smiling. "I don't know. I was hoping maybe we'd kiss before you made such a mess of your face"

"Oh, is this a problem for you? Here…" I lean over and wipe my mouth on his shirt sleeve.

His other arm closes around me, wrestling me away. Giggling, we topple backward onto the bed, him a little underneath me. Our eyes meet. And then I'm rolling over on top of him, pinning his arms over his head. His mouth parts in surprise, and I see his Adam's apple bob. Everything else goes very still.

My body warms, acutely aware of his own frozen beneath me. I can feel his pulse racing where my hands hold his wrists. When he tries to lift one, I let him. His fingers settle on my lips and then trace their way back to my ear, gently tucking a strand of hair that's gotten in the way. His touch is electric, more than ever before.

In my suspended moment of bliss, his face changes from awe to desire. His chest rises to meet mine, and his free arm folds around my waist, rolling me over so that now I'm the one with my arms over my head. His hands run up the length of them until our fingers intertwine.

"Kaylin," he breathes.

I nod, letting him know the answer to his unasked question. Who knows when we will get another chance like this? He uses his foot to kick the bedroom door shut.

As he presses his lips gently on mine, the chaos and terror of this world fades, and all that matters is the two of us, here and now. I wiggle my hands free from his grip and clutch his strong shoulders as our lips move together with more urgency than I ever imagined possible. My fingers work their way up into his hair, deepening the kiss until I can hardly breathe. His heart hammers against my chest, and I know he's just as desperate as I am for more. Now.

The camper door wrenches open and frantic steps pound their way inside before we have any time at all to untangle.

"Kaylin?!" My mom's frantic voice echoes in the tiny space beyond the bedroom door.

Groaning, Farren rolls off me and sits up, helping me do the same. We straighten our disheveled clothes, cast each other mournful looks, and rise. Farren opens the door and steps out first, smoothing his hair down.

"Leeyah?" he asks, letting a little irritation peek through his tone.

"Thank goodness," she says, pushing past him to grab my hand as though I'd really gone missing or something. "They've found us."

CHAPTER THREE

"I'm sorry," Leeyah insists, cheeks flushing in admission that she knows what she's interrupting. "I was hoping to give you a bit of normalcy for your birthday, but the world doesn't seem to want to cooperate."

"How much time do we have?" Farren asks, peering out the small side window.

Leeyah takes my hand and starts toward the door. She looks over her shoulder at Farren. "Nance and Gareth spotted movement about a mile out. The threat's on foot but heading toward our location."

I follow Leeyah outside, trying to ease my hand loose. I'm not a child anymore. As of today, actually. "Any of these vehicles have fuel?"

"They're all dry. We need to move. Now."

I'm disappointed but not surprised. Fuel is becoming harder and harder to come across of late. If it's not already used, then the precious gas has evaporated.

Farren rushes out the camper and slings his pack over his shoulder. "What's our exit?"

Leeyah points east at a low mountain range on the horizon. "There's a trailhead a bit into the woods. I don't think we're going to have time to clean this location. But we need to make sure we erase our tracks that lead to that trail."

A pattering of footsteps catches my attention. Amanda races up to me. "Sorry, Kay, I hoped for a more relaxing night for you."

This world sucks. Every chance I get to be a normal girl, chaos returns and chases everything good away. I kind of want to scream and throw a tantrum as though this were my eighth birthday instead, but I force a gentle smile for Amanda. I don't want her distracted by negative feelings tonight. The most important thing is that we all escape.

The soft blue moonlight creeping through the sporadic clouds illuminates the others gathering in front of the small rest stop building. Leeyah gestures for us to head over there too. Farren draws his pistol and checks the clip for ammo. He clicks it back in and nods at Leeyah. She follows us over to the building with arms spread out like a mother hen herding her chicks. Everyone but Nance and Gareth are already milling about, anxiously checking their supplies. Leeyah will radio Nance with the location to meet up at.

Off to the side, I spot Ava and Envee talking with Jax. As Leeyah and Farren discuss our exit strategy, I make my way over to Ava.

She places a hand on my shoulder, her dark eyes narrowing on me. "We can't keep running from these sector groups. They're not going to stop hunting us."

"I know," I say, feeling like a broken record. "But—"

Jax steps toward me. "It might be time to do what we discussed a few days ago."

I suck in a sharp breath. One of the most important things I've learned from Jax is that we do *not* use our Push ability on innocent people. But this life of always being on the run and always having to look over our shoulder has worn down that resolve. For him, anyway. I'm not so sure if I'm ready to bend that rule.

Ava, on the other hand, has always believed our ability is the next step in human evolution, and that being able to tap into the collective consciousness gives us the right to help shape a better future for everyone. For her, that means using our Push on innocent people with no abilities of their own. Jax might be shifting sides on the subject, but the slope still feels too slippery to me.

"What are we talkin' about?" Stratton says in a mock whisper as he creeps up behind us.

I straighten and pivot toward him. "Oh, hey... nothing. Just talking strategy."

Jax removes himself from our huddle without saying a word. Losing his parents was one thing but having their former evil henchman as part of our group has not been easy for him. Ever since we met, Jax has been the most forgiving and open person I've known, but I'm afraid that's changed since Seattle.

Stratton raises up his hands. "Seriously, when is that dude going to stop holding a grudge against me? I didn't kill his parents."

"Stratton, please," Ava snaps. "You need to be careful with your words. You might be on our side now, but you were at the center of a lot of horrible things that are still fresh in people's minds. Just watch yourself."

Stratton lowers his eyes a bit. He has to realize that Ava is probably the last person he wants to mess with. One of the many things she's referring to is the death of her partner Maddux. While the blood isn't on Stratton's hands personally, he was one of the main reasons we all wound up in that situation. It's a testament to her will power that Stratton's made it this long.

"Time to go guys," Farren says, walking up and thankfully breaking up the awkward situation. "Nance and Gareth are only five minutes out. That means the Southern Alliance's group is not far behind."

We gather our supplies and head into the woods, Farren and Caiden cleaning our tracks as we go. Nance and Gareth will lead Billy Wilson's fighters down a different direction before cutting back to meet with us.

Leeyah sets the pace. Overgrowth has nearly concealed this trail, but we manage to navigate its narrow path as we head up further into the hills. The scent of fresh pine is overwhelming. The fragrant, wild aroma reminds me of traveling through the Sierra mountain range as I avoided the former Magnus Order. The beauty of the world still exists despite the disgusting nature of its inhabitants. We are heading towards the Cascade mountain range. These remote areas are safer than the people-infested cities, but resources will be even more limited. We should have looted more stale snacks from the store.

Switchback after switchback on this jagged path takes its toll on my legs. After about half an hour, the foliage becomes much denser. Tall evergreens stretch up to the night sky above, as if the massive trees desperately yearn to kiss the stars.

Upfront, Leeyah raises a hand, signaling for us to stop. A much-needed break is in order. Just in time, if you ask me. Our group spreads out and finds tree stumps and boulders to sit on. Just as I settle on a mossy rock of my own, I spot Leeyah waving Farren and Caiden over to her. Curiosity lifts my tired butt off the boulder and carries me over to them, feeling mildly annoyed I wasn't waved over as well. There's no need for Leeyah to treat me with kid gloves. I'm no less integral to the missions just because she's here.

"We better make sure," Leeyah says darkly. She glances at me with eyes full of regret. . "Let's get Jax and Envee to expand their awareness in the area."

"No problem," I say in my best soldier voice.

My suddenly overbearing mother turns to Caiden. "Get a couple guys and set up a patrol around our camp."

Caiden nods, but his eyes say he still thinks it's overkill. "On it."

We break our huddle and jump into action. Farren squeezes my hand, letting me know he picked up on my frustration, before heading off with Caiden. Leeyah smiles at me and makes her way back to inform the others what's happening now. I shuffle through the camp searching until I see Ava and Envee sitting on a toppled over oak tree. Just off to the side of them, Jax leans up on a granite outcrop, staring off into the darkness.

I brusquely inform them of the situation, and without hesitation, they all prepare their Push. We've been doing this for a while now and have become quite good at surveilling expansive territories. We stand in a half-circle and expand our minds to envelop the greater landscape. Envee rests a narrow hand on each of Jax and my shoulders, her energy flowing through us, sending goosebumps down my arms.

Shadows of life pop into my inner vision just as quickly as they fade. My attention zips past the scurrying, simple creatures that swarm this area. I'm looking for a specific consciousness, one that I've felt before—Gareth or Nance. My awareness flows from me at a rapid pace with the help of Envee's amplification.

Moments pass as Jax and I push the limits of our reach into the surrounding forest. I'm about to reach the furthest my awareness can extend, when a dotting of human life trickles into my inner thoughts, grabbing my attention. The familiar vibrations of Nance and Gareth wash over me. Like an embrace from a family member—you just know who it is. I'm pulled back from their conscious essence when I notice a large group of other humans flanking them from all sides. The same dark fear that consumed me that day at the Lost Souls shelter when I was only eleven radiates down my spine. Billy Wilson has my friends.

CHAPTER FOUR

THE OTHER INFLUENCERS and I find Leeyah scurrying around the camp, checking on our people one by one. She spots me and quickly sidles up to us. Stratton, who was trailing behind Envee, quickly aligns himself next to my mother. I'm going to have to have a talk with him about this new obsession of his.

"Nance and Gareth were captured, weren't they?" Leeyah says without missing a beat.

I sigh and nod. "They've got them held up at the very edge of our collective reach. It's like Billy's group knows our capabilities."

Leeyah plants her hands on her hips. "Yes, they want to draw us out, all while keeping a wide perimeter."

I pan over the makeshift camp, hoping to spot Farren, but he has not returned from patrolling with Caiden yet. A hollowness forms in my chest. I want him safe and by my side.

"What do we know of their tactics?" Ava asks Stratton. "The Vernon Society must've dealt with them plenty during their reign."

I glance at Jax, who stands to my left. His head dips at Ava's mention of his parent's former home.

"I never dealt with the other ally groups," Stratton says, shifting his sights from person to person. "That was Miya's thing."

I stretch up to get a better view of everyone and spot Miya sitting next to Ray and Erin. They have always been tasked with keeping watch on her. Their long experience with the Protectors has prepared them for this sort of duty. Leeyah calls to Erin and gestures for her to bring Miya over. Erin slaps Miya on the shoulder, urging her to get up and move.

"Is that necessary?" Miya says to the fit and serious fighter.

Miya straightens her fitted, pleated top and gathers herself before walking over to our gathering with Erin close behind.

She looks at me. "Will you tell your mom that I'm part of this group? I'm on your side. Haven't I proved that with all the intel?"

Leeyah steps closer to her and tilts her head down to make eye contact with the slender, height-deficient woman. "I'm sorry, but we have to be careful. We don't have the luxury of making mistakes anymore."

"I get it, I do," Miya says without hesitation. "One day you guys will have to start trusting me, though."

Leeyah purses her lips. "We'll see, but right now we need more of that intel."

"Alright, what do you need?"

"I need to know their combat tactics...strategies in the field. Do you know more about how Wilson operates?"

Miya combs back her straight, dark hair with her fingers. "Well, I don't know everything, but I know he is brutal. He spares no expense when it comes to completing a mission." She glances at me before turning back to Leeyah. "If he's after her...and with what she did to him...I have no doubt he'll do whatever it takes to make her suffer."

I frown, wondering who's been filling in the blanks of my story to someone we aren't sure we can trust. Maybe she overheard Amanda explaining it to Ava and Envee. I can't imagine Amanda and Miya sitting down for a cozy chat at my expense.

"He's still just a man," Stratton says. "He doesn't have our powers. Let's take this fool out."

Miya rolls her eyes at him. "It's not going to be that easy. Not only do they all have the implants, but I'm sure he's fully aware of all of our capabilities. From what I've heard, he is completely obsessed with eradicating Influencers. It's why he's moved up the ranks so fast."

"So, basically I've created an elite Influencer Hunter?" I ask no one in particular. "Great."

My heart sinks deep in my chest. Killing has never been my thing, but I'm seriously regretting leaving him alive all those years back. Not only does he threaten my existence, but now everyone I care for is at risk.

Leeyah paces back and forth in front of us, debating the options that must be running through her mind. She stops and pivots to face us. She's about to say something when Farren and Caiden burst through the outer thickets into our clearing. Caiden stumbles but catches himself on his knees. He stays like that, panting for air. Farren is also breathing hard and sweat runs down his forehead. I hurry toward them, and the rustling of feet in leaves tells me the others are close behind.

"What is it?" I ask, grabbing Farren by the shoulders. "What did you find?"

Farren grimaces as he looks up to the night sky trying to regain his composure. Finally, he locks eyes with me. "There's more...than one... hunting party...out there." He takes a few deep breaths. "We put all our focus...on Wilson's team. The Southern Alliance is coming at us from all sides. They have us surrounded."

Leeyah rests a hand on top of my hand on Farren's shoulder. "How much time do we have?"

Before Farren can answer Leeyah, Jax steps up beside of me with Envee grasping his wrist. "I just shifted my awareness away from Wilson's group to the greater area. We've only got a few minutes."

Leeyah lifts her head. "Everyone... They've found us!" she shouts. "Arm yourselves and find cover. Set a perimeter. Go now!"

The camp explodes into action. Erin and two of the other remaining Protectors, Ray and Ryan, set up a chokepoint near the trail, rifles at the ready. Miya huddles behind them. I spot Amanda grab a pistol and take cover behind an outcropping of tall trees. I want to rush to her side and protect her, but she knows what she's doing. We've been at this way too long now. Caiden moves over to flank her, easing my concerns a bit.

Farren straightens and turns to Leeyah. "Are you sure we shouldn't move out...try to draw them deeper into the woods?"

Leeyah shakes her head. "It's too late it seems. We need to make our stand here."

Jax agrees, and he and Ava take Envee to a canopy of brush behind Erin's group. They will do what they can, but if everyone from the Southern Alliance has the implant, they will be limited. I'm the only one with an ability that can affect more than just people.

Farren jumps into action. "Alright, let's get you two under some cover." He points to a ditch near the back of the makeshift camp. "There...that will provide a little bit of cover and give me a vantage point for whatever comes. Let's get both of you over there and hopefully Kay can do her thing."

Leeyah nods, and we sprint over and slide down the shallow incline to take cover. Dust kicks up and thorny twigs scrape the exposed skin on my legs. Ignoring the pain, I steady my nerves. I don't have much time, but I need to see if there's any animal support nearby.

Farren checks the ammo clip from his pistol and pops it back in. "I'm shooting anything that enters."

With only the faint light from the moon, our Influencers will have to be our eyes and watch out for anyone closing in.

Leeyah places her hands on my cheeks, resting her forehead on mine. "Don't worry, I'll watch our awareness. You focus on those beautiful creatures out there."

She pulls back and smiles. I return the smile, albeit faintly, and quickly sit back against the berm of the pit. I close my eyes and instantly enter the invisible fold that surrounds reality. Like a blurry dream, I wade through the haze and search for the pops of pure light that only innocent animals have. Besides the occasional hiding mouse, there isn't much near our camp. We need larger reinforcements. I exhale a deep breath and push out my reach further.

Seconds pass and bright halos of white light filter through my awareness. A large pack of coyotes scavenge about half a mile out. That'll have to do. I don't have time to hunt down the more ferocious bears and mountain lions.

I close in on the pack and just as I'm about to enter their minds, a dark vibrating cloud spits out tendrils of smoke all around my vision. I pull back my consciousness, but I'm locked in my extended state of reality, unable to return to my true form.

A heaviness weighs on my perception, and the light from the coyotes dims and fades out, leaving me alone with whatever this dark presence is.

"I see you," a deep guttural voice enters my mind.

My awareness rattles, a wave of fear expanding over this conscious state. I can somehow feel my real body shiver with anxiety as terror pours over my real-world form.

"I see you," the voice repeats.

Confusion courses through my mind, but curiosity wins out. *"Who are you? What are you?"* I plead, unsure if the presence can even hear me.

The plume of smoke retreats and is absorbed into a bus-sized ball of spiraling darkness that ripples as it rotates just a few yards before me. The surrounding reality is gone, replaced with an endless white nothingness that stretches out for as far as my mind can reach. I feel nothing but this heavy presence.

"I am what is next, what is meant to be." The spiral vibrates in unison with each word.

Farren's face enters my inner mind. *"I don't understand, where am I? My friends need my help. Please let me return to them."*

"He is not one of us," the voice says plainly, somehow reading my thoughts. *"You are more, we are more."*

This thing's riddles are starting to annoy me. Anger bubbles from within. *"You need to let me return to my people. They need my help...please."*

"Not everyone is your people. This you know."

"Please, I don't have time for this," I beg, trying to break my Push.

"A discussion will take place," the deep voice echoes. *"I will bring our kind to safety."*

"Wait, what do you mean. What are you going to do?"

The orb doesn't respond. The large mass of smoke stops spinning and falls, exploding into grey mist before I'm left alone in the empty whiteness.

"Hey, wait! How do I get out of here?"

There's no answer. I remain in this void. Panic fills my thoughts, and I try to focus on my Push, hoping to bring my awareness back to the current reality. Disconnecting from the greater consciousness is as simple as having a desire to take a breath with my actual lungs. That yearning to feel my physical body usually draws me back to reality. But right now, I feel separated and alone.

My inner mind scans over every corner of this vast white space, but there is nothing until an orange and red brightness expands before me. A hot fiery ring tears through the whiteness forcing me to look away. The sensation of warmth tugs at my awareness. In an instant I am pulled, my inner-being torn atom by atom as I'm sucked through the opening.

A flush of floral-scented air washes across my face, forcing my eyes to open. The empty white is replaced by the endless stars dotting the dark sky above. I quickly lean forward and slam my hands to the gravelly surface below. I'm back to the current reality. I crane my neck in both directions to regain focus of my surroundings and spot Jax, Ava, Envee, Stratton, and Leeyah laying on the ground just feet from me. They stir as they seem to be regaining consciousness.

"What the hell?" Stratton asks, grabbing the back of his head as he sits up.

Jax shuffles over to me. "Are you alright? What happened?"

"Wait, where are the others?" Leeyah pleads as she pulls herself off the ground to stand.

Envee moans as she comes to. Ava scoots over to comfort her, wrapping her arms around our youngest Influencer's shoulders. Ava studies our surroundings and shifts her attention to Leeyah. "This is not the camp."

I glance at Jax and start to stand. He quickly takes my hand and helps me up. My heart sinks as I realize Farren, Amanda and all the others are gone. "No, this is not the camp. Someone... or something moved us away from the oncoming danger."

Stratton pops to his feet and smooths back his dark bangs to better lock his eyes on me. "Um, what are you talking about?"

A shudder runs through me, remembering. "I wasn't alone in my Push. There was something powerful in there with me."

CHAPTER FIVE

"We've got to find them," Envee cries out.

Ava wraps an arm around her shoulders. "We'll figure this out, don't worry."

Leeyah looks me up and down, checking for injuries. "Okay, what's going on? How are we here..." She eyes our surroundings. "...wherever we are?"

Panning over the landscape, I notice the terrain has changed very little. It's the same towering evergreen trees, sporadic overgrown brush lining narrow trails that lead out in all directions. We have to be in the same general area, but I have no idea how far we are from the others.

"Something took over my Push," I say, shifting my gaze from person to person. "Whoever or whatever it was...it was dark, and it wasn't like anything I've seen before."

As confusing as the experience was, I go over every detail I can remember from my odd encounter. No one really says anything as they try to process what I'm telling them.

In his typical blunt way, Stratton breaks the silence. "Okay, so wait, this *smoky* ball or whatever transported us away from our camp to save us?"

"I know about as much as you do..." I say to Stratton. "...and to be honest, I can't even think about this anymore. We need to find the others."

"Alright, alright," Leeyah states, waving her hand to gather the group's attention. "Envee, Jax, see what you can find. We need to get our bearings. We'll figure out what happened to Kay after we get our people back."

I hate having my family broken up again. Amanda, Farren and the others don't deserve to suffer while we are whisked away to wherever. Unsure of what to do, I pace back and forth, trying to wrap my mind around all of this.

Ava walks up to me. "I know these types of people. Wilson wants you and he's going to keep our friends alive until he gets you. But he won't have a chance. We're not going to let them hurt anyone."

I stop and face the dim horizon. "I don't know, this doesn't feel right. And now I have to worry about whatever this thing was in my Push."

"Are you sure it's evil or bad or whatever? Why would it save us?"

Leeyah shuffles up to us and looks at Ava. "Just because something might not be evil doesn't mean it's not a threat to us. All I know is that we have each other, and no matter how connected our existence is with the world, we're still individuals experiencing life the best we see fit." Leeyah pivots to meet my gaze. "And because we have our individual freewill, humanity is all about strengthening the personal connections we've made. We protect our own first, then we protect the world."

Ava and my mother have always had a bigger picture mentality of the world and Influencer abilities. They're able to disconnect from their personal emotions in order to see the greater reality, but right now I just want to make sure Amanda and Farren are alive.

"They're about a mile west," Jax calls from behind us. He and Envee dart over to join our gathering. "But there's a hell of a lot more people around them now."

A heaviness lodges itself in my chest, tightening my breathing. I'm sick of this never-ending life of living on the run. Even when I find people that I care for, nothing ever changes. Someone's always out there trying to control me or kill me.

"I've got an idea," Jax says, distracting me from my inner thoughts. "But it might not be the most popular idea."

"What do you have in mind, hun?" Leeyah asks Jax.

Stratton's eyes flit to Leeyah, a sense of longing washing over his face. He yearns for those terms of endearment that she has for Jax and me.

Jax turns in the direction of our captured people. "We give Kaylin to them."

Stratton, laughs, nearly choking from apparent shock. "Nice! Welcome to the dark side, yoga-boy."

"Shut up," Ava snarls, stepping up to Stratton.

Stratton takes a step back from Ava's frigid stance. "What? It wasn't my idea."

"Hold on, hear me out," Jax says, breaking the tension. "We need to set up a diversion so we can take them by surprise. If Kay gives herself up, we can walk in there as a group and take advantage of the chaos to get our people out."

Leeyah shakes her head firmly. "I don't like this. It's way too risky. Wilson and his people could just shoot us all down on first sight."

"He won't," I say. "He will want his moment with me for what I did to his brother. He will draw it out as long as possible just to make me suffer."

Jax places a reassuring hand on my shoulder. "We just need to be close enough to use the block disruptor that Miya acquired from our Talas strike." He pulls the small handheld device out of his pocket and raises it up for all of us to see.

Back in Lost Souls, our resident genius, Owen, gave me a quick and dirty lesson on this tech. The makeshift device is nothing more than a trigger connected to a battery with wires and copper coils that creates a simple magnetic burst in a small radius which disables anything that uses electricity to operate. That includes the bioelectrical powered implants that prevent Influencers from manipulating those that carry them. It's not permanent, though. Unfortunately, it only lasts until the implant can recharge from the bio-energy the body generates.

During the takedown of the Magnus Order, Miya was able to acquire one of Owen's devices from us before her betrayal. She revealed it to our group after the Vernon Society was eradicated. It was her attempt to build our trust by handing over something that she knew could disable the small implant that she and Farren have lodged in their necks from their former lives in the Order.

Unlike the larger device that helped us win the battle with the Vernon Society in Seattle, these handheld devices have a small radius. With Wilson and his fighters all being implanted, it is our only chance of opening their awareness to our Push abilities, giving us a small window to free our friends.

Leeyah crosses her arms over her chest, standing firm. "It's still too risky. We're not doing that. I won't put her or any of you at risk like that."

"Mom," I say, shocking myself as I've never called Leeyah that before. "Um... It's...uh, my decision, no one else's. It's my mess, I'm going to clean it up."

Her hardened brow softens at my words and she pauses for a brief moment. "Kay, I can't lose you again. Please, there has to be another way."

Jax's soft blue eyes narrow as he straightens up. "With the numbers they have out there, there's no way we can get close. It'll be a bloodbath. I don't want to do this either, but Wilson has more of our family out there too. Family is more than blood."

His words hit my core like a sack of rocks. Jax allowed his own parents to die because he needed to protect more than just blood. There was more at stake and he was able to make the hard decisions. If he didn't, we would've all been dead by now.

"All right, how do we do this?" I ask, looking over our group.

Jax and Leeyah go back and forth with strategies and tactics for several minutes before they finally address the rest of us.

"Alright, the plan is fairly simple," Leeyah says softly. "Simple, but by no stretch of the imagination is it easy." She cranes her neck to look at Stratton. "You're going to turn her over to them. You're going to act like you had a change of heart and you have to do what's in your best interest."

Stratton scoffs and rolls his eyes. "Do I ever get to play the part of a good guy?"

"If the shoe fits..." Ava smirks.

"Shut up!" Stratton snaps.

I raise my hands out. "Guys. Enough. What Leeyah is proposing makes the most sense. There's no way they're going to believe we all just decided to walk in and give up."

Jax slaps his hand on Stratton's shoulder. "Brother, you're one of us now. You can do this."

Leeyah steps close to him. "I believe in you. But this is still your call."

Stratton swallows and diverts his eyes from my mother. "Okay, fine, I'll do it." He clears his throat and straightens his shirt. "Besides, once we activate that disrupter, I finally get to stretch out my Push muscles and have some fun."

Stratton might put up a wall and act like he doesn't care, but over the last few weeks, I've seen a softer side of him. He cares for this group, my mother in particular, and as much as that annoys me, I believe he really wants a better life for himself. That includes having people he can trust around him.

After a bit of recon around the area, the plan is set. Leeyah, Jax, Ava, and Envee will take the high ground just east of Wilson's group and wait for the surrounding awareness to become open for manipulation. Stratton and I will stroll right up to them. I'll be held at gunpoint. Probably my least favorite part of this plan.

As we prepare to leave, Jax and I scan over the area just to make sure there won't be any surprises. True to the Southern Alliance's nature, there are no Influencers being forced to work with them. These extreme fundamentalists truly hate our kind. And that will be their downfall.

Checking her rifle's ammo, Leeyah turns to me. "I'm not comfortable with any of this. First, you tell me there is some kind of mysterious presence in your Push, and now I'm letting you walk away from me right into the arms of the enemy. If I lose you..."

"Mom, I know," I say, avoiding her eyes. "This plan will work. It has to."

She smiles and reaches for me. "I like the way that sounds. I never thought I would hear you call me that. All those years searching for you, I just wanted to see your sweet face. Having you call me Mom makes this very real. Just be careful and keep your awareness open."

I accept her hug and let my own arms fold around her back. Suddenly, I grasp a little tighter than I expected. "I will, I promise. Now, let's get our family back."

Using the cover of night, we head down into the lush but darkened valley toward our enemy. The lower we travel, the denser the forest becomes, providing a much-needed canopy to hide under. We've been trekking downhill for about thirty minutes now. My knees burn, but I fight to keep pace with the others.

Besides the scurrying of animals, there's no one. None of Wilson's people have entered my mind yet. Based on what I've seen of the gear his people carry, I have no doubt they have surveillance equipment to keep an eye on their perimeter. So, we have to be extra careful to not be spotted too soon.

We reach a narrow gully about a quarter mile out from their camp. Leeyah, Jax, Ava, and Envee reluctantly say their goodbyes before splitting off to take the high ground to prepare for our next move. Stratton enthusiastically accepts a hug from my mother and less enthusiastically a handshake from my cousin. A lot of this plan relies heavily on how he plays the betrayal out.

Watching my mother walk off up the dusty side trail yanks on my heart, throwing me right back to the emptiness I felt when I was alone at my first shelter in Lost Souls. Amanda's gentle face enters my mind, steadying my resolve for what I'm about to do. She would drag me through a blinding dust storm in the middle of the barren Lost Soul's wasteland before letting anyone hurt me. But it's Farren's warm eyes that dig at my soul and shudder my breathing. I long for another chance to finish what we started earlier. Tonight's not the end of our story. Our group has to overcome this—no matter the cost.

"Let's move, you filthy prisoner," Stratton says, playing up the stupid smirk on his face.

I grin and shake my head. "Yeah, yeah, let's go."

I take one last look at the trail that Jax, Ava, envy, and my mother took. Nothing but the settling dust remains. Turning back, I catch Stratton gazing in the same direction, his eyes wide. He notices and quickly diverts his stare.

He starts down the path toward Wilson's forces, but I catch up and match his pace. "Hey, so, I haven't had a chance to talk to you in a while. Must be an adjustment being around all of us, yeah?"

His jaw tightens. "Why, because I'm evil and you're all angelic freedom fighters?"

I grab his wrist, forcing us to stop. "Will you stop that? None of us think that...well, maybe Ava, but, yeah, that's gonna take some time." I flit my eyes from him and gather my thoughts before meeting his gaze again. "If there's anyone that knows how this world can suck, it's me. I don't hold your past against you. And honestly...I can't tell you for sure that if I were in your shoes, I wouldn't do the same thing. It's how you act when around good people that defines you."

I release his wrist and his mouth forms a thin line, conflict filling his eyes. "Maybe so, but your Push isn't dark like mine, you don't know how it feels to do what I can do."

We start back down the narrow path, deeper into the dense forest. He flicks on a small pocket flashlight as the overhanging foliage dampens the dim white light from the stars that seem to canvas every inch of the night sky. The lack of city lights or burning fires free the stars to pour onto our helpless little world.

"My Push might not be as harsh as yours..." I follow the staggering light his flashlight projects onto the trail. "...but I've felt what you do. I know how it can consume your mind. You're strong. Not many people could hold those powers and not go crazy in the process. You didn't let the darkness win; you found the light and you've found a family."

His head turns slightly, but he doesn't look as all the way back as he walks a step in front of me. "Maybe," he says. "I envy you and what you have." He laughs. "That sounds stupid with how *awesome* our current situation is, but no matter where we are, you have so much love that surrounds you. That, I doubt I'll ever have."

A weight lodges itself in my chest. I feel guilty for begrudging him Leeyah's affection all this time when I only just now opened myself up enough to call her Mom. "I don't believe that. Give it time, everyone deserves to be loved."

We don't say much for the next ten minutes as we focus our awareness on finding Wilson's people. At the fray of my reach, pinpricks of activity flutter and expand. I slow down and tug on Stratton's shoulder. He stops and pivots to face me. "What is it?" he asks, scanning over the blackened tree line.

My Push extends much further than his can. I study the conscious reflections that filter through the muddled landscape in my mind. Like shadows with no forms casting them, the awareness of what feels like one hundred people emerge through my murky awareness.

"Oh, crap," I stammer. "This might have been a dumb idea."

CHAPTER SIX

"This just got real," Stratton whispers, picking up on them too.

I scurry to get in front of him. "Get that pistol out and pointed at me. Just make sure your finger is not on the trigger and the safety's on."

We start playing our parts as we move closer to our deadly stage. Stratton knows to hold off on using the disruptor in his pocket until Wilson and enough of his goons are within the radius. We need enough free minds to create a diversion.

I shorten my strides to walk closely with Stratton. "We're each other's leverage, so stay extremely close to me. You're not expendable if my life's at risk. And they're not going to do anything stupid if you have a gun pointed at my head."

My breathing becomes heavy as we close in on Wilson's people. Beads of sweat trickle down my forehead, and my palms become clammy. I guess I don't need to pretend to be scared for our little ruse. I'm terrified for real.

"Stop where you are," a deep man's voice echoes through the dark landscape we walk toward. "Put your weapon down!"

Stratton jumps into action and wraps his forearm around my sternum, nearly choking me. "I'm not dropping anything! I've brought your commander something he's been looking for. My weapon stays with me and so does the girl until I get what I want."

Beams of light cascade to life from the tree line before us. One after another until more than a dozen flashlights flood the area. I lower my gaze as my eyes adjust. Stratton pulls me in closer, the barrel of his pistol jabs into the back of my head. A brief moment of doubt floods my mind as I hope Stratton can maintain his composure and pull this off.

Three people emerge from the trees. Light flickers as they cross through them, casting an eerie shifting silhouette. I lift my head and squint, trying to focus on them.

"Well, this is interesting," a deep scratchy voice says. "Lower your weapons, boys. Looks like our job just got a hell of a lot easier."

The man struts up closer and his scarred face comes into focus, a sinister grin inching up on his mug. Billy Wilson.

"That's far enough," Stratton demands. "This isn't my first rodeo, whatever the heck a rodeo is. I have something you want, but it's not going to come cheap."

Billy tightens his grip on his assault rifle. "What's stopping my men from just plowing you both down where you stand? Maybe you didn't fully think this through."

"I'm not stupid," Stratton snarls. "I know what this girl means to you. All I have to do is pull this trigger and your evil revenge plans or whatever go out the window." Stratton taps the barrel of his gun on my head. I wince and shoot a glare at him. Stratton continues, "What's it going to be? Am I going to ruin your fun or you going to hear me out?"

Billy locks his brown eyes on me and stares for a few seconds, not saying a word. I swallow hard but refuse to be the first to break this little staring contest.

Billy blinks slowly and diverts his gaze from me to Stratton without moving his head. "Well, looks like you've done your homework. What do you want?"

Stratton's chest rises and falls as he leans on my back. "Let's get out of this creepy forest and we can discuss things at your camp."

"Alright then." Billy smirks and raises his hand out, gesturing for us to follow them.

Stratton straightens. "Keep your people in front of me. If I sense anyone's awareness trying to sneak up on me or targeting me, I end her. I've got this area covered."

Billy slows but continues down the path before us. "Ah, so you're one of them. Do I know you?"

It was probably not smart for Stratton to let the fact that he's an Influencer slip. But we can't let Wilson and his people think they can just pick us off with a sniper from a distance. These people need to know that our awareness can sense their movements.

"I would hope you've heard of me," Stratton says, keeping a few yards distance between they're people and us. "I would think my reputation would have reached your little sector group. We were once allies. Leo Stratton ring a bell?"

Billy flings his rifle over his shoulder and it hangs across his back. His men flank him, weapons at the ready. He peers over his shoulder before returning his gaze to the front. "Oh wait, you were one of the Vernon Society's attack dogs, right? I think I've heard of you. You're that dark freak that messes with people's minds and emotions. It was you and that girl Influencer, whatever her name is, that prevented us from simply taking over your pathetic little group. Look at you, trying to make something of yourself on your own now."

Heat radiates from Stratton's arms and chest, his anger burning. He squirms a bit, and I sense that he's about to lash out on Wilson. I can't let that happen.

"So, this is what you've been up to for all these years since last time we spoke?" I say in an even tone. "Looks like your Southern Alliance finally took you back. I guess you just needed a little nudge to get back in line."

Stopping hard, Billy spins on his heels, rage hardening his scarred face. "You want to do this now, girl?" He flits his eyes to Stratton, who shifts the gun to the side of my temple, reminding the Commander what's at stake.

Billy takes a slow breath in and blows it out his pursed lips. "We'll have plenty of time together after my little business arrangement here with this other freak."

Billy doesn't say another word as we walk for several minutes through the spiraling trails that lead into the woods. Flickering light dances between the tree trunks as we approach a break in the foliage. Stratton's death grip on me lightens a bit as we follow Wilson and his men, but his gun stays trained on me.

Dozens of people enter my awareness as we near Billy's camp. Even though I can't interact with Farren's consciousness, due to the implant, I desperately search for his familiar and comforting essence. Every muscle in my body contracts as fear and anticipation wash over me.

We walk past two massive redwood trees that act like a gate as we emerge into a clearing. Several fires radiate and illuminate the large opening. Dressed in the same riot gear that Wilson wears, dozens of men and women mill about. Several large tents line the back of this clearing and butt up against the tree line.

I desperately pan over the faces swarming around us, searching for Amanda, Farren and the others. They're nowhere.

Stratton slows, pulling me back with him as we lag behind Billy. Stratton's breathing has picked up. His hot breath warms the back of my neck. This can't be easy for him. We are a target for dozens and dozens of highly trained fighters.

Two large men rush up from each side, their rifles locked on us. Billy quickly raises a hand and tames their approach. He waves them off and they obey without a single word. More and more people from this camp shift their eyes to look at us and stop what they're doing. There's a stifling tension in the air.

"Please, follow me," Billy says in a less than enthusiastic tone.

Stratton hesitates for a moment as he analyzes his surroundings, but eventually we start walking toward one of the tents that Billy is leading us to.

Just as we hoped, Billy's fighters begin to surround the Commander's location. He's well protected and that's exactly what we need—as many of these people within the disruptor's radius as possible.

A man with a thick beard and emotionless expression holds the flap of the tent open as Billy and two others walk in. The grizzly man eyes Stratton and me and gestures for us to follow.

Stratton once again pulls me in tight and digs his weapon into my temple, playing up the only thing keeping us alive.

My heart races and wants to rip from my chest. I can only hope that Farren, Amanda, and the others from our group can take advantage of our distraction. Ava and Jax will create enough chaos to give them a chance.

Billy sits on a small unfolded stool as we enter. He grabs a hunk of dried meat from a small sack next to a backpack stashed near the rear of the tent. Billy bares his yellow-stained teeth and gnaws off a piece and chews slowly as he glares at me. Swallowing down the way-too-big bite, he raises his brow and widens his eyes as he shrugs at us. "Well? What's the plan here."

Playing up the frustration, I thrash around in Stratton's arms, before pretending to give up. "Why don't you guys just let me go and then you can kill each other?"

"Shut up," Stratton snarls. "You're in no place to talk here, honey."

Ouch.

Even though I know this is an act, I'm not a fan of being treated like crap.

Billy sighs and folds his strong arms across his broad chest and stares at Stratton. "So, what do you want? Let's get this over with."

"It's pretty simple. I want a pack filled with food and supplies and free pass to the Canadian border."

Billy tilts his head. "Well, that sort of goes against what we're doing here. Ya see, your kind is on the endangered species list." Billy jabs his finger in his mouth and dislodges a chunk of his snack from his teeth and flicks it onto the ground. "If I go letting one of you free, what kind of message is that sending to the rest of you disgusting freaks?"

Anger boils inside and forces its way out. "Is this really all about me? I mean, you bullied me, and I was just protecting myself. I was just an eleven-year-old kid. I'm assuming your brother, Alex, didn't survive? I'm sorry, I really am, but all I was doing was trying to protect myself. You attacked us first, remember?"

Billy jumps to his feet and stomps over in front of us. Stratton pulls us back a step and shifts the barrel of his pistol from Billy to me.

Billy's breathing becomes heavy and he balls his hands into fists. An intense scowl fills his face. "Don't you ever say that name again. You think you're so innocent. Your kind is an abomination. God didn't make you, science did. You use those evil abilities to kill my brother. And you're going to suffer for it."

I shake my head. "I was born just like you were. I had parents. I wasn't created in some lab. I didn't ask for these abilities. I didn't ask to be hunted my entire life."

"Well, it's simple," Billy says in an even tone. "A life for a life."

Stratton clears his throat. "Are you two done? This is boring. Let's get back to it already." He pats my head like a dog on a leash. "So, if you want her alive for whatever sick games you have planned, I'm going to need that deal. Can we make this happen now?"

"Let me ask you something," Billy says, looking at Stratton. "Where are the others?" He points at me but keeps his eyes on Stratton. "Where's her mommy and the others like you two? You want a deal, I'm gonna need them too."

I freeze and hold onto my last breath, fear locking my body.

Stratton remains quiet for a moment as Billy shrugs, waiting for an answer from him. My pretend captor looks down at me over my shoulder, confliction overtaking his steady glare.

Stratton trains his sights on Billy. "This wasn't part of our plan, but what the heck, I am what I am. The others are about a quarter-mile east in the hills. They're waiting to strike."

"What the hell, Stratton!" I crane my neck to glare at him. "We trusted you." He wraps his forearm around my neck and locks it in place. "I'm never going to be a part of your little group. No one's going to fully accept me. I have to look out for me."

One of the two men who stand guard at the tent's entrance moves up to our side. Stratton steps back to get a better eye on him, maintaining his now real death grip on me.

"Sir, should we prepare the team?" The heavily armed guard asks.

"Yep," Billy says. "If this freak's telling the truth, then we've got a deal. Go get my squad and wait for me outside the tent."

The guard nods and lumbers out of the tent. My anger boils inside. Fearing for the safety of my mom and the others, I thrust my elbow deep into Stratton's midsection. He groans and drops to one knee, releasing his grip on my shoulders. I start toward the tent flap when Billy cocks his pistol, stopping me in my tracks. Slowly, I turn and see his weapon pointed directly at me, a sinister grin spreading across his face.

My throat locks, preventing air from entering my lungs. *This is it, I'm dead.*

I turn my head, not wanting to witness what's about to happen when Stratton quickly leaps between me and Billy.

He's grimacing from my strategic blow but has regained his composure. "Now, now," Stratton urges. "If you want the location of the others, I'm going to need her alive still."

Billy's remaining guard inside the tent blocks the now-closed exit, his rifle firmly pointed at me. The tension in the air is thick.

Billy releases a heavy sigh and lowers the barrel of his weapon. "Killing the both of you would be so easy right now. But I have a bigger purpose in life. I need those other influencers dead. Give me their exact location and you get what you want."

As if on autopilot, my awareness opens up as dozens of people converge outside this tent. I'm about to give up once more when the pliable being of those around us becomes fully accessible to my reach. Their implants have been disabled.

My eyes widen as I look at Stratton, who smirks with pleasure at his apparent use of the disruptor.

I pivot to look at Billy, but his attention is on the empty space above my head, confliction filling his eyes.

"What the hell is going on?" Billy pleads.

The commander drops to his knees, tears streaming down his eyes. He's unable to control the flow of emotion as it paralyzes him. Ava has him. He's reliving his worst memory. Guilt swirls in my gut. I caused that.

"Alex, no," he cries. "Not again. Brother, please."

Several pops of gunfire outside the tent pull me away from Billy. I catch Stratton with his eyes closed, clearly extending his Push out onto the exposed fighters. I grab his hand and drag him out of the tent, past the guard who's curled up in a fetal position, crying uncontrollably.

We burst out of the tent into the open where chaos reigns. Broken bodies lie all over the ground. A loud burst nearby draws my attention to a man as he falls to the ground, his weapon smoking in his hand and a bullet hole gushing blood from his forehead. Others run in terror all around, their inner fears overwhelming their minds. Those who are outside of the disruptor's radius are consumed with confusion as they try to stop the madness that is happening all around them.

"Hit them again," I urge to Stratton. "See if we can open up more of their minds."

Stratton shakes his head, rattling his focus back into place after his Push. Digging into his pocket, he pulls out the handheld device. He clicks the trigger, but nothing happens. No electrical zip or anything. After several more unsuccessful clicks, I remember these devices need to be recharged after one use.

"Crap," I blurt. "I forgot it's one and done. We need to move. Let's find the others."

He nods, stuffs the disrupter back in his pocket, and we dart to the edge of the camp, sticking to the shadow's edge. Stratton drifts in between his conscious reality and his extended push. I'm unable to open my awareness to search for our people, as I need to help guide Stratton out of here while he's dealing with the now exposed Southern Alliance fighters. I'm going to have to look the old-fashioned way—with my eyes.

Some of the Alliance's fighters are taking drastic measures to save their people. With the butt of their rifles, they are knocking out those consumed with Stratton and Ava's darkness. Heavy thuds followed by the toppling over of armed guards consume the camp. Fighter after fighter drop and the chaos slowly begins to ease. My heart races as we're running out of time. The distraction is waning.

Stratton and I reach the backside of the camp behind the far tents where we finally find four armed guards standing over our missing team. They all sit in a circle in the dirt, weapons trained at their heads.

I spot Amanda near the middle of the group with Farren in front of her, his eyes locked in determination on one of the fighters. Caiden, Miya, and the others fidget in place. They want to make a move, but it would be suicide if they did.

"Can you reach anyone still conscious?" I ask Stratton. "I need you to send someone in there to give us an opening."

"I'll try."

Stratton yet again closes his eyes and focuses on what he needs to do. Frantically, I look over the camp for anything that might help. I notice a man writhing in terror on the ground, his rifle a few feet from him.

"Stay here," I say to Stratton. "I'm going to get us a weapon."

Stratton opens his eyes and nods, but quickly closes them to refocus.

Crouching down, I scurry into the tall grass and then drop to my knees to crawl closer to the man. I'm just a few feet away when I hear someone shout at me. Craning my neck, I see a slender woman holding an assault rifle that's pointed right at my head.

"Don't move, you freak," she snarls.

I drop back and sit on the ground, raising my hands up. "I just want my friends back. Please, let me go."

She cocks her head to the side and grins. "Are you stupid? I'm going to complete the mission even if my commander couldn't."

She stiffens in her stance and grips the weapon tighter. My breathing quickens, and I struggle to keep my eyes open. The woman's gloved fingers hover over the trigger when a guttural scream comes from behind her. A terror-induced fighter charges our way, a pistol locked in his hand.

"All influencers must die!" he screams.

The woman spins to cut him off, but the apparently influenced man doesn't hesitate and unloads several rounds at the woman. Her head flies back as thick blood splatters the ground in front of me. Her body falls like a board, lifeless. The crazed man charges at me as I shield myself with my arms, expecting the worst. He races right past me and heads toward our people. It's Stratton's manipulated reinforcement.

Electricity pulsates through my body as I grab the pistol off the ground and pop up to run after the influenced man. Breathing heavily, I eject the weapon's clip to make sure it's not empty. I slap the clip back in and raise the gun, locking my arms, ready to act.

I rush past Stratton who's crouched down in the nearby tall brush, still concentrating on his Push. If I didn't already know he was there, I would have never seen him in the low light. I don't want to leave him there unprotected, but I have to get to our people and help however I can.

Just up ahead, the armed fighters guarding our people notice the man rushing toward them. They shift their weapons from my friends on to the frantic man.

"Hold it right there," the guard in the front demands, pointing his rifle at our manipulated distraction.

The terrorized man doesn't stop and runs frantically forward. Two stocky guards break from the group to head off the man. I keep a safe distance and stick close to the tent off to the side. Farren notices me and sits up, his eyes widening with concern. Nance and Ray also notice me and look at each other. Something inside tells me that they're going to make a move and take advantage of the situation.

The influenced man reaches the oncoming guards and fires a couple of rounds just past them. Ducking to avoid the aimless gunfire, the men quickly return fire and pelt the man with bullets until he drops.

Hands bound behind their backs, Nance and Ray jump to their feet and drive their shoulders into the heavy-set woman and the lanky man who are distracted by Stratton's diversion.

Erin, Gareth, Caiden, and Farren make their move to help Nance and Ray. They overwhelm the two guards with sheer bodyweight, crushing them to the ground.. Amanda hangs back with Miya on the ground and shifts to one knee, ready to move.

With the crazy threat neutralized, the two guards who broke from the group spin on their heels and charge toward the altercation. Their weapons raised, one of the men targets Farren while he's wrestling with the ties that bind his hands. My jaw drops as fear flushes my entire body. I grip the pistol tighter and without hesitating unload several rounds. The powerful weapon recoils, forcing me to close my eyes from the blast for a second.

When I open them, both of the charging guards are face down in the dirt, just a few feet away from my friends.

I cup a hand over my mouth and lower my weapon. I just killed two people in cold blood.

The guards on the ground try to clamber up while their attackers are distracted, but Farren drives a knee into the lanky man's gut, forcing him back down. But then Farren can't resist looking at me, his eyes checking on me, knowing how horrified I must be.

Grimacing in pain, the guard takes advantage of Farren's misplaced attention and pulls out a small blade from his belt. I try to call out to him, but terror grips my throat and the words don't escape.

Farren tilts his head and narrows his brow at me, confused by my reaction. Waving my hands like a crazy person, I watch in what feels like slow motion as the man drives his weapon at Farren. Before the blade reaches him, Ray lunges forward. The blade drives right into his chest.

Farren is knocked back by Ray's body as it crumples to the ground.

Farren writhes on the ground, frantic to get up. His hands bound behind his back make it difficult. The lanky man pulls his blade from Ray's lifeless body and jumps to his feet. He heads straight at Farren. Shaking in terror, I raise my pistol once again, but before I can fire, Nance drives his head right into the man's temple, dropping the guard to the ground, unconscious.

With all the guards neutralized, Farren struggles onto his feet and awkwardly runs to me. I drop the pistol and jump on him, nearly taking him down. Unable to use his bound hands, he buries his head into my shoulder.

Farren pulls his head up to meet my eyes. "Are you alright? Are you hurt?"

Emotion consuming me, I'm unable to speak and simply nod. Tears stream down my cheeks. and I refuse to let go of his shoulders.

"We need to move," Stratton says as he runs past us. He meets the others up ahead and starts cutting the bindings on everyone's wrists.

I take a deep breath and wipe the tears with my sleeve. I pull out a small pocketknife from my belt and grab Farren's hands to cut the bindings.

Farren rubs his now free wrists and drops his head to meet my gaze. "He's right we got to go. Now."

CHAPTER SEVEN

CAIDEN SLINGS RAY'S body over his shoulders as we move deeper into the darkened woods. Shouts and screams fade the further we trek. Farren holds my hand, pulling me along as my other hand grips Amanda's. I don't want to be separated from either of them.

Stratton leads the group as we make our way back to Jax, my mom, and the others. I feel bad for doubting his intentions back at Wilson's camp. Stratton might be an abrasive person, but he really saved us all back there.

"So what the hell happened?" Amanda asks, pulling herself closer to me. "It was like you guys just blinked out of existence. We searched for you, but then Billy's people found us."

"Yeah, I thought I was going crazy," Farren adds. "Where were you?"

I shake my head, gathering my thoughts. "I'm not sure what happened, but there was something or someone who took over my Push. I think it was trying to save me and the other Influencers. I really don't know how it happened."

"Well, that's just crazy," Amanda says. "I swear, my life is definitely never boring around you."

I offer her a soft smile. "I'm just glad we were able to get you guys back."

Farren massages his thumb on the back of my hand. "So, do we need to worry about whatever this thing is?"

"I don't know. I haven't felt it since. One crisis at a time."

Farren nods. "Well, maybe you shouldn't be alone when you use your abilities?"

I offer him a smile. "Maybe."

We follow the dim glow from Stratton's flashlight for another twenty minutes or so. Amanda walks up ahead with Miya now. Farren dutifully stays by my side. I keep my awareness open, searching for the familiar conscious spirits of the others. Stratton's been doing the same as he guides us in the general direction where we split up from the others. With the overhanging trees, the darkness is disorienting, making normal navigation impossible.

I take a break from scanning the area and catch Farren staring at Ray's limp and bloody body bumping against Caiden's back up ahead. Squeezing his hand tighter, I lean in to meet his eyes. "Hey, you okay? I'm sorry about Ray. He was a good guy."

Farren takes in a deep breath before slowly releasing it through his pursed lips, holding back his emotions. "He sacrificed his life for me, and honestly, I barely knew him. I'm getting real tired of this life."

I wrap my free hand around his arm and rest my head on his shoulder. "I know what you mean." Swallowing hard, I shift my gaze down to the trampled path our group is creating. "I think I'm getting numb to killing. I killed two people today, but my mind seems to want to ignore that. What does that say about me?"

Farren abruptly stops, forcing me to hold onto him to maintain my balance. He narrows his sights on me. "It's normal, Kay. Your mind is protecting you. This world will not allow any of us to keep our hands clean." He once again looks at Ray's body as Caiden continues to move forward.

Empathy for Farren's grief cuts through my own numbness. Killing someone who threatens you or your friends is much different than having someone sacrifice his life to protect yours.

Those upfront stop at the narrow creek that cuts off our path. A peaceful trickling of water distracts my mind from what happened at the camp. Stratton pivots to face the group. "Jax and the others are close. Let's grab a quick drink of water before we head up to them."

No one argues with him, especially Caiden, who has been struggling to carry Ray's body through the rough terrain. He gently places him down off to the side of our group and drops to the ground, exhausted. Amanda brings a freshly filled canteen to him, and he grabs it and guzzles it down, water dribbling down his neck. He smiles at her before tossing the container to Farren.

Once we meet up with the others, we'll give Ray a proper burial. My mom has lost so many from her team.

Guilt starts to weigh on my soul. Everything she's done has been for me. So many have died, and we have nothing to show for it. We're still on the run, struggling to stay alive.

Farren leads me to an outcropping of small boulders near the stream. We take a seat, my legs instantly thanking me.

"Can you make sure we haven't been followed?" Farren asks, handing me the canteen. "I'll be right here."

"Yeah, sure," I say, taking a long sip of water from the one canteen we've all been sharing. I hand it to him, and he tosses it to Gareth.

I take a deep breath and fall back into my Push. The darkness of the forest fades and the dots of pure bright light trickle in before my mind. Expanding beyond our immediate location, I scan over our surroundings and find no one is approaching from the direction we just came from. We're in the clear. I shift my attention and verify that Jax and the others are nearby. Maybe ten minutes out.

I'm about to withdraw from my Push when that familiar, scratchy voice returns from inside my awareness. *"I am not done with you...further discussions will be had."*

Not wanting to be trapped inside my Push again, I instantly recoil and burst awake into the reality where Farren is sitting next to me.

"What happened?" He asks, taking my hand.

My breathing races with unease, and my jaw quivers with fear. "That thing returned. I didn't stick around this time."

Farren draws me in close and wraps his arm around me. "I'm here, I've got you. You're not alone. What did it say?"

"It, um…it wants to communicate with me." I stare up to the thick canopy above, trying to regain my steady breathing. "I don't know what to do. It won't leave me alone."

Rubbing my back, Farren tempers my anxious energy, bringing me back to a stable place. "Alright, alright…I don't think you should use your Push until we figure this out, okay?"

"I don't know. I need to help the group—everyone's relying on me. Without my abilities, I'm useless."

"That's not true," Farren insists. "You're a leader. Your decisions have changed the country. If it wasn't for you, none of us would be here. We'd all be stuck serving some manipulative sector group."

More of us would be alive if it wasn't for me.

"I don't know," I say. "I'm not going to sit back if I can help. That's not me."

Farren obviously doesn't agree with my decision, but he knows who I am. Nobody's going to tell me what to do. I love him, but not even he can change that.

"Well, please just avoid using your Push alone," Farren pleads.

I stand and gaze around the group before turning to look back at Farren. "I'll try. Let's just get everyone moving. I'm sure the others know we're close. We need to create some distance between our group and Billy's. He's going to be pissed after things settle down at his camp."

Farren takes over for Caiden and carries Ray the final stretch. After another fifteen minutes of hiking through this dense wilderness, we reunite with my mother and the others in a small granite quarry at the base of a dense forest that leads to the mountain range on the horizon.

Leeyah wastes no time and finds a beautiful spot that overlooks the valley for us to bury Ray's body. There isn't much time to say anything with Billy's people still hunting us. My mother and her remaining people are devastated at the loss. Her Humanity's Protectors were once a large group that fought for those affected by corrupt sector groups, but now all that remains are my mother, Nance, Gareth, Ryan, and Erin.

My mom gathers everyone together at the top of a large outcrop of boulders that overlooks the valley below. "We need to find somewhere to get some supplies and regroup. We've gotta get out of this forest." She points to a dim glow of yellow light off in the distance. "There. That's the closest sign of civilization. We need to get there, find what we can, and get out. Wilson's people will know that we need to get supplies, and I am sure he will turn over every rock to find us."

Walking close to the edge, Caiden trains his sights on the town. "That's at least a mile out. My knees are going to hate me, but let's go!"

***

Sticking to the outskirts of the town, about a hundred yards out, we evaluate our surroundings. This place is nothing more than several trailers and temporary structures surrounding an inner camp. Several lights dot the perimeter so they must have a generator or a solar and battery system in place. We need to be careful. Anyone that has working electricity will be well-armed to protect it.

"I'm sensing about a dozen people," Leeyah says to our group before turning to Jax. "Jax, what do you got?"

Jax folds his arms. "Same."

"Do we knock and say hello or just storm the place?" Caiden asks no one in particular as he checks his rifle's ammo.

Our desperation has forced us to be a bit less cordial when dealing with new settlements. We won't use force, but we will scope things out without asking first. There's no telling who's sympathetic to the Influencer cause. Most people just want nothing to do with us. They fear the repercussions from interfering with the sector groups' collaboration to eliminate our kind.

"Let me try something first," Leeyah says to Caiden. "It's been a while, but I think I can do it."

"Mom, what are you talking about?" I ask.

Leeyah pauses for a moment before stepping into the center of our gathering. She narrows her eyes on me, trying to focus through the limited lighting. "You remember me telling you about my ability? I think it would be wise to try it. We don't have time to interact with these people."

My mother's ability goes far beyond altering the mood of conscious souls. When she was younger, she was able to, in a sense, freeze time for those affected by her Push. She could slip within the pockets between their conscious state while those people remained stuck in their current moment.

"When was the last time you were able to do this?" I ask, trying not to sound too much like I'm condescending to her age.

Stratton plants his hand on his waist and straightens. "Does someone want to fill me in on what they're talking about?"

Leeyah moves into the middle of our gathering and smiles at Stratton. "If I can still call on it, my ability will basically pause the reality of those affected, allowing us Influencers to just step around their awareness."

"Damn, that's cool," Ryan says, scratching his thick greying beard. "You never told us about this before. It could've come in handy for the Protectors."

Leeyah combs back her matted bangs with her fingers and faces Ryan. "Ever since I found Kay and Jax, my ability has been re-energized somehow. I can't fully explain it but now is the time to give it a try."

"What do we have to lose?" Gareth asks. "Us non-Influencers will set up a perimeter and keep an eye out for the Southern Alliance as well as anyone at this settlement."

Billy's people took our weapons when they captured our group. All we have is one rifle and a few handguns that we looted from Wilson's fighters before we took off. Avoiding conflict would be wise with our group so vulnerable.

It doesn't take long before everyone agrees, and we decide to try Leeyah's plan. We divide the weapons amongst the non-Influencers and they spread out to monitor this camp from a safe distance. Envee stays back with Ava to watch the greater area. Jax, Leeyah, Stratton, and I gather to approach the settlement.

I nod at my mother, offering my full confidence in her renewed Push ability. She returns the gesture and quickly shifts to face the settlement. Her eyes close and a calmness seems to wash over her entire body as she takes in a deep breath, slowly releasing it.

A sense of ease seeps into my body as well, all anxiety melting away. The subtle rumblings from the settlement have stopped, leaving an eerie quietness.

Leeyah's eyes flutter open. "It worked," she says in a flat tone. "I'm not sure how long I can hold this Push though. Let's get in and out as fast as we can. Look for weapons, food, and water. Only take what we need. Leave enough for them to survive. We don't want to leave these people vulnerable."

My mother's eyes are wide and focused. She's struggling to hold the Push, but she is determined to make this work. She's truly unbelievable. I wonder what it means that being near me and Jax makes this possible for her. Or is that even it? What if this has something to do with the strange voice in my Push? I shake off the thoughts. No time for that now.

We move in quickly from behind a long, busted up trailer home. We round the corner and spot a group of four women stuck in mid-stride, completely unaware of their delayed state. A middle-aged woman with auburn hair smiles at a shorter woman whose joyous expression makes me curious about what they were discussing.

Jax steps past me and draws my attention to a skinny guy wearing a tank top at the outer edge. This kid is not much older than me. Strapped around his narrow shoulder hangs an automatic rifle. I shift to the opposite side, across the inner opening of this camp where another young guy seems to be patrolling with a shotgun.

Shielded by RVs and dilapidated temporary structures, the inner camp seems to be where these people live out their lives. From what I can count, there's about fifteen people stuck in time around this camp.

"Enough sightseeing," Stratton snaps, breaking me from my aimless evaluation. "Grab some food from that storage truck over there." He points to the right of me. "It's open. I can see some cans and boxed food."

My mother sidles up to me. "Pretty crazy, huh? It used to scare me, and I would never use this ability when I was younger. I regret that. I could have done so much good when I was your age."

"It's amazing," I say with a wide grin.

We walk together over to the open storage truck and climb in. I'm having a hard time not looking at the amazing effect of my mom's Push. But with her diving right into these boxes, I follow her lead and rummage around. She starts filling an empty cardboard box with all sorts of canned fruits and vegetables. I toss in some dehydrated meat packs and rations. We're careful not to take too much. We just need enough to get moving. These people need to survive just like we do.

"Alright, that's enough," Mom says. "From what I can see they have plenty to spare. Let's find Jax and Stratton and get out of here. I can feel my grip on these people slipping."

We hop down out of the truck and grab our box of food. I spot Jax walking over to us with a couple pistols and a few hunting knives in his hands. He carefully sidesteps the statue-like people and meets us back where we entered. Not as thoughtful, Stratton lumbers over, nudging into an older man, nearly knocking him over. Stratton grabs the guy's shoulder to steady him before he turns back to us and shrugs. He has the automatic rifle and shotgun strapped over his back along with a few boxes of ammo.

It's going to be so odd for these people after they snap back to reality.

"Are we good?" Jax asks.

Breathing a bit heavier now, my mother looks at the boys. "You guys didn't take all the weapons, right?"

Stratton shakes his head. "Nah, they have quite an arsenal of hunting rifles back there. They won't miss any of these."

"That's goo—" Mom starts, before dropping to her knees and grabbing her head with both her hands.

I quickly drop the box of food and tuck a forearm under her armpit to steady her. "Mom?! What's the matter?"

Stratton and Jax crouch down, their eyes wide.

"Something's different," Mom says through gritted teeth, her eyes clenched tightly shut.

Without a sound, my mother vanishes, popping right out of existence.

I topple over on to where she once knelt. "No, what the… Mom? Leeyah?"

"Not good, not good," Stratton snarls.

"What the hell?" An unfamiliar deep voice shouts from across the camp.

The settlement bursts back to life, people dazed and confused. A woman screams as she spots us.

"We need to run, now!" Jax orders.

"No! My mom?! We can't just…"

Jax doesn't let me finish my jumbled mutterings. He quickly helps me up and throws the pistols and knives in the box and hoists it into his arms.

Fear encircles my mind. My mom is gone. With no other choice, we rush out of the camp and into the darkness.

CHAPTER EIGHT

MY LEGS BURN as we trample through the uneven forest floor. Farren, Amanda, and the others follow us blindly, unaware of what just happened to my mother. Every step away from where I last saw her is a knife in my heart, but we have to get some distance between us and that settlement.

Jax raises a clenched fist, finally signaling us to stop. I hunch over, lungs begging for air. We're surrounded by tall trees, well away from the settlement. Armed and ready, Caiden, Gareth, and Nance take positions at the edge of the trees, keeping an eye out for anyone that's followed us.

"What... the hell... is going on?" Amanda struggles to catch her breath as she narrows her eyes on me. "Where's... Leeyah?"

I stand taller, regaining my composure. Peering over the exhausted group, I take in a few deep breaths. "I think whatever took over my Push earlier, took her. It's like she popped out of existence."

Jax steps closer and rests a hand on my shoulder. "Whatever happened, stopped Leeyah's Push and brought those people back to their reality. We had no choice and had to get out of there."

"You just left her?" Erin accuses.

"No!" My voice cracks.

"She left us," Stratton snaps, awkwardly patting me on the shoulder. "Were you listening or not?"

"But she didn't want to," I correct, squeezing my eyes shut as memories of her pain face flood my mind. "I'm telling you it was the same thing that took us before."

"You have to find her," Erin grabs my arm roughly. "Use your ability… get in there and bring her back. We just lost Ray. We can't lose Leeyah too."

Farren comes to my side and gently pries Erin's fingers off of me. "Hold on, hold on." He raises both palms out. "We don't know what we're dealing with. We can't expose Kay to whatever this is. We have to be smart."

My chest tightens, emotions spilling over. I swallow them back and let out a slow breath. "I'm going to find her. I just don't know how yet." I look over the concerned faces that surround me. "I'm not about to lose her now."

Jax sidles up to me. "I agree that Leeyah must be found, but we need to find somewhere to regroup first. The Southern Alliance is still out there, and this settlement is probably on the hunt for us now as well." Jax pans over each of the Influencers in the group. "I think we'd better not use our Push abilities until we get somewhere safe. We can't afford to expose any more of us."

"I agree," Ava says and turns to me. "We'll figure this out, but we need to be careful." She grabs Envee's small hand and looks down into her frightened eyes.

Every part of me wants to just dive into my awareness and search for my mother, but they're right, we need to be smart and not risk losing anyone else.

I nod to Ava. "Okay, let's find somewhere to camp and figure this out."

"I believe there's a network of ranger outposts lining these mountain ranges," Ryan states as he points in the direction of the towering foothills.

My heart sinks at the mention of the ranger outposts. The last time I was at one of them I unleashed the full force of my ability to manipulate animals. The primal carnage I released onto the people hunting me was terrifying.

"Good idea," Farren says to Ryan before shifting to me, eyes filled with understanding of what I went through. "We might be able to find some maps and information about this terrain. Plus, we just need to find a spot to rest up and decide on what to do next. We won't stay long."

Jax points up to the faint ridgeline in the distance. "Alright, let's head up and get a better lay of the land. There should be tracks near the top that will eventually lead us to one of these outposts."

As he takes the lead, I feel a faint spark of something like happiness in my heart. Everything is terrible, more than it's ever been before with Leeyah gone, but it seems like Jax may finally be emerging from the shell that losing his own parents sent him into. If we can count on his leadership again, there may be hope for us yet.

**

It must be midnight now. Traversing up these darkened trails that never seem to end has sapped whatever energy we had gleaned from the adrenaline rushes of our two daring escapes. We're all moaning and groaning now. Without Leeyah to keep us in line, it seems we're all reverting back to babies as sleep fights for control of our minds.

But we walk on. Jax, Farren, and Miya have been leading us through the dense forest. As former Magnus Order personnel, they have more experience than anyone in our group with mountainous terrain and networked outposts. Amanda has been by my side the entire hike, but neither of us has had the energy to really talk. We just want this night to be over with.

The sloping trail levels off suddenly, and we pour out onto a worn and overgrown dirt road.

"There," Miya says, gesturing up the road a bit. "A road marker."

We all move closer and spot a rusted post holding up a small sign etched with faint lettering.

Farren examines the sign and turns to face the group. "Before things went to crap, the government would use these markers to help rangers manage the outposts. There should be one about a quarter-mile east."

Caiden grunts, and without waiting for anyone else, he charges forward toward the outpost. He's clearly done with this nature adventure and just wants to be there already. None of us are far behind him. Walking on this level road is much better than the uneven trails we just ascended so we arrive at our destination in no time at all.

"There it is," Farren says, turning back to check on me.

About thirty yards up to the right in a carved-out clearing stands a large two-story building with cement walls and a metal roof. This is much bigger than the outpost I had the pleasure of staying at last time. Caiden, Erin, and a few others scope out the structure's surroundings before returning to the group.

"It's all clear," Caiden says to Farren.

We make our way to the main metal entrance. Jax checks the handle, but it's locked.

"Nope," Caiden says, shaking his head. "Oh, we're getting in this mofo. I'm not sleeping in the dirt tonight."

"No gunfire," I say to Caiden. "We have to keep a low profile." I turn to face the others. "Anyone know how to pick a lock?"

Several people raise their hands which isn't surprising. This is the freakin' apocalypse after all.

It only takes Gareth a few minutes of fiddling with the lock before it is busted open and we have access to the ranger outpost. Those with weapons enter first just to be cautious. Moments later, Farren emerges from the entrance and waves the rest of us in.

A stale coolness washes over me when I enter the structure. I nearly sneeze as a dusty scent tickles my nose.

Panning over the room, a fairly large work area with two long tables takes up half the space. Two sectioned off rooms with open doors, on the opposite side, make up the rest of the lower level. A couple of cabinets line a wall next to a narrow staircase.

We waste no time and rummage through the cabinets. Amanda pulls out a medkit and a hand-cranked lantern. She spins the handle several times before flipping the power on. The light flickers but eventually remains constant, illuminating the entire lower level.

I'm having a hard time keeping my mind off my mother's disappearance but digging through the other cabinet helps me focus. I find a stack of thin blankets stuck on one of the lower shelves and pull them out.

Miya scrambles down from the second level. "There's a big space up there with six cots and a bathroom. No running water, though."

Jax walks up to me at the cabinet and touches my shoulder. "Hey... I know you're thinking about Leeyah. I am too, but everyone's exhausted and it's extremely late." He pauses for a moment. "We should let everyone get a few hours of sleep and then try to find your mother at first light."

I shake my head and avoid looking at him. "I don't know. Wherever she is, she's alone, and maybe even trapped in her Push like I was. She might not *have* a few hours."

Jax pulls his hand from my shoulder with a heavy sigh. "I know, I know. I can't make you not look for her, but please understand, we are much stronger as a group. Envee is already out." I follow his gaze to the corner of the room. Envee is asleep in Ava's arms as they rest on the ground. Jax turns to look at me again. "I don't think our efforts will be as effective if we are all exhausted."

He's right. If we go looking for my mother, and we aren't at full strength, we could lose more of us to whatever is out there.

I take a moment to answer him. "Okay, you're right, let's try to rest up."

He nods and moves away to hand out the food we got from the settlement to the group.

I hand over the blankets to Ryan who takes them upstairs. Farren finds me and smiles. He takes my hand and guides me to the second level. The metal stairs clank with every heavy footfall. My ankles don't want to work anymore. We reach the top and Farren tugs me toward a free cot.

I shake my head. "Let's save it for the others. I'm fine on the floor."

Farren tilts his head down at me. "No way. We're going to need you at full strength tomorrow. I've got first watch and will be back up here in a couple hours. Now, rest up, please. It *is* still your birthday." He gives me a rueful smile.

With a tired laugh, I lean my forehead on his chest. "I don't think so."

"It still counts." He kisses the top of my head. "Now sleep."

My body doesn't put up any more fight, and I topple onto the makeshift bed. I drop my head back on the thin pillow. Farren pulls a blanket over my lower half and smiles at me before heading back downstairs.

I keep replaying what happened to my mother. Each time I see her clutching at her head, my heart squeezes painfully. Several minutes pass as more and more of our group fill the remaining cots and open floor spaces. It feels like I will never fall asleep, but minutes later my eyelids abruptly refuse to stay open, and I drift off into the abyss of my mind.

***

I stand alone in the forest. Tall, thick tree trunks surround me like a fortress wall. Confused, I try to remember how I got here, but my mind is slow and unfocused. I should be terrified, but there's a calmness in the isolation. The wind rustles the branches above, soothing away my worry. I look up, but only a faded darkness fills my vantage. How did I get here?

Spinning in place, I analyze the wooded backdrop. Nothing makes sense. The trees are all identical in size and position, evenly spaced apart. Beyond the unnatural tree line, there's nothing but more oddly similar trees. Yet still, my nerves are unfazed.

"Kaylin!" A distorted yet familiar voice calls in the distance.

I jump into action and run toward the voice. Cool air rushes past my face, but the scenery doesn't change. It's like the forest floor is following me underfoot, keeping me in the same spot somehow. I stop and spin around, looking for the ranger outpost, but instead my mother stands several yards out, behind the unrelenting barrier of trees.

Perfectly aligned between a small gap in the identical tree trunks, my mother smiles at me. She's wearing a flowing white gown that dances around her like tendrils of silky smoke. I don't feel any wind. The air is calm and motionless.

"Mom?" I call out to her. "What's going on? Are we in a Push?"

Her smile fades, and she gazes over her shoulder. I step forward to see what she's looking at, but those damn trees refuse to cooperate, maintaining my limited vantage point. Nothing makes sense here.

Leeyah turns back to me and her eyes widen. "Don't come for me. It wants you."

I shake my head and glare at her. "Mom, I'm not going to leave you. Please come to me." I reach out to her.

"Please, let me go," my mother says looking over her shoulder again.

I step toward her again, but I only make it a few feet before her white outfit explodes like evaporating steam. Just as quickly as the whiteness fades, dark rippling smoke wraps around her.

I drop to my knees and try to scream, but nothing happens. My voice is gone… and so is my mother. All that remains is the ominous ball of swirling darkness as it hovers in the distance.

My arms are locked by my sides, and my body no longer has the will to stand. The presence vibrates and expands, consuming the trees. But all I can think of is my mother as the forest fades into black smoke. The smoke inches toward me. I close my eyes and refuse to give in.

A pull tugs on my core, and I flash my eyes open.

The wooden beams and metal roof fill my view. All the emotions that refused to exist in the forest rush into me all at once, stealing my breath. I roll over off the cot and onto the floor, thudding my hands and knees on the wood planks. I gasp for air.

"Kay?" Amanda's voice filters closer. "Are you alright?"

Her hands grab my shoulders. I crane my head to look up at her, my breathing steadying. "It has her."

CHAPTER NINE

FLICKERING LIGHT DANCES off the condensation clinging to the pine needles at the top of the tree line. The morning air is cool and steady. I pull my arms in close and fight off the goosebumps. Farren and Caiden are discussing something on the other side of the dirt tracks across from the outpost. It doesn't look like they are agreeing on everything.

Ava, Amanda, and Jax stand with me at the opening to the structure. After what happened early this morning, I don't think they want to leave my side.

Inside, Nance and Miya hand out rations and cans of beans. After our makeshift breakfast, we will pretty much be out of the food we took from the settlement.

Ryan and Erin are out patrolling the perimeter, making sure the Alliance's thugs are nowhere near us. I can only worry about one thing right now. If I don't figure out a way to get my mother back, I don't know what I'll do.

"Sweetie," Ava calls from behind me. "Did you eat yet?"

I don't turn around to face her and simply shake my head. "Not hungry."

"Well, I'm saving you a ration pack for when you are."

Amanda slips her hand through my arm and pulls herself in next to me. She feels warm against my frigid, exposed forearm. I glance down at her and offer a simple smile.

Keeping my eyes trained on Farren and Caiden, I watch as Caiden shrugs and walks off. Farren shakes his head and turns to look at me. He narrows his eyes and starts walking over.

"Well, he's a joy." Farren rolls his eyes.

"What were you guys talking about?" I ask him.

He once more shakes his head. "You know him. He's all gung-ho with you and the others using your abilities to find your mother." Farren looks at Jax over my shoulder before turning back to me. "I'm not willing to expose you and the others. There has to be a better way to find Leeyah. Whatever that thing is that took her, it's way too dangerous for you to go in blind."

Scowling, I fold my arms. "I told you it's not your decision if I use my ability to find her or not."

His brow lifts. "I know, I know. I just want to do whatever we can first before we expose you."

"Kay, please," Amanda says, squeezing my arm. "Just let us try to protect you before you go all agro on this thing."

They are the closest people in my life, but sometimes that can hinder my ability to do what's right. If what my vision or visit or whatever it was is real, then that thing wants me, and it took my mom to get to me.

"Sorry," I say through gritted teeth. "But I'm going in."

***

Everyone's finished eating, and even I decided I'd better have some food, or I won't have the energy for what I'm about to do.

Erin and Ryan have returned from their old-school, non-Influencer patrol. They didn't see any signs of Billy Wilson's group or anyone from that settlement. We've kept off their radar for now.

The other Influencers and I have moved to the upper level of the outpost to prepare. Ava is not allowing Envee to be a part of the search for my mother. While I know her special ability would come in handy, I agree with Ava. We shouldn't put a child in danger like that.

Even though Farren has the block implant, I can somehow feel his nervous energy radiating from him as he stands guard at the top of the staircase. He wants Leeyah back, but not if it means losing me.

Jax drags a couple folding chairs over to the center of the space. "Okay, we need to keep an eye out for each other's awareness. Like we discussed, only Kaylin will search for Leeyah. The rest of us need to watch the collective consciousness." He places the chair down and turns to me. "If things get out of hand, we all need to pull out and check on each other."

I nod and take a seat in one of the chairs. "Just give me time to find her."

Stratton kneels down across from me. "I'm not holding back if this thing gets aggressive. Although, I'm not really sure how to attack a *mind monster*."

"Just focus on the mood of the Push," Ava says to him as she takes a seat in the other chair. "Make sure we are fully aware of everything going on. We can't have any blind spots in there. Just be alert."

Jax kneels down next to Ava and glares at Stratton. "There's no such thing as monsters. It's got to be a person. An Influencer with extraordinary ability. So, just like with any other Influencer, we can sense and alter its Push."

"Let's just do this, please," I say to no one in particular. "You guys are my tether. Stay locked onto my conscious radius."

Stratton shifts on the floor to get comfortable and flits his eyes to me. "Just don't get all *Kaylin* on us and leave us behind with your mad skills."

I smile and shake my head. "Just keep up, okay?"

"Sure thing, boss."

I ignore him and look at Jax. "I'm going in."

Jax offers something like a smile. His lips twitch anyway. "All right, we've got your back."

Like with every Push, I close my eyes and concentrate on the greater surroundings of my awareness. Reaching out, I quickly sense the others entering my consciousness. Their familiar presence puts me at ease.

Pushing farther out, all I find is the familiar scurrying of wildlife that fills this forest. Through the blurry haze of my mind's interpretation of reality, the radiating white light of the animals give me a greater sense of how far my Push is reaching. Like an expensive horizon of shadows and vibrations, the animal's bright light flickers through. Amongst the scattering of wildlife, I search for my mother's unique essence. I long for the comfortable ease her awareness radiates. Her presence has always felt like a tight embrace from a loved one—unconditional and warm.

As I extend my push, the once-strong tether from my friends starts to thin. Only Jax's ability can match my reach. I don't want to leave them behind, but I need to find my mother.

Pulling back a bit, I settle my awareness on the edge of Jax's strong vibrations. Before we started, we discussed Jax being a link between my Push and Stratton and Ava's. Jax will need to split his attention between me and them.

Turning my focus onto the greater expanse beyond my reach, I scour the distorted landscape of consciousness. The farther I reach out, the more darkness fills my state. Even my connection to the pure essence of wildlife in this area begins to dim the harder I push.

After several minutes of focused searching, I begin to tire, and my ability begins to falter. I push hard to maintain my connection to the area, but I can feel the consciousness slip out of my mind's grasp. I'm about to pull out to take a short break when a cloudy form emerges far off in the distance. The heavy thuds from my real-world heart echo into my conscious state. The shadows that represent the conscious landscape fade and dissolve into thin air, leaving just a dark horizon and the undefined presence.

"Mom, is that you?"

As if my internal words trigger something, the entity flickers between wisps of white smoke, only to be instantly engulfed by dark clouds once more.

I'm not sure how, but I can now feel the ominous entity that has been tormenting me. There's a weight that pulls on my chest that roots me in place. The heaviness feels overwhelming and unrelenting.

"Where's my mother?" I demand.

The blurry cloud of smoke spins, tightening its form, returning to its familiar spiral of pulsating darkness. As soon as it does, the horizon brightens. All the texture of my inner consciousness fades, leaving only the empty white backdrop and the unknown presence. But this time something is different. I still feel the faint tether from Jax behind me. Whatever happens, I need to hold on to that connection. It might be my only way back.

"*Impressive,*" the familiar raspy voice resonates from all around me. "*Not how I intended. Not normal.*"

An inner energy sparks within my mental core, fueling my determination. "I said, where is my mother?"

The tendrils of dark smoke spin faster around the orb. "*Mother with me. Power from her different. Must feel what is new.*"

"What are you?" I plead.

The ball of darkness slows to a gradual rotation. "*I am you. I am mother. I am all.*"

My patience wanes. "What the hell does that mean? Why do you speak in riddles?"

"*Forgive. Awareness has been unconnected from what you call reality for much too long. Words spoken, not required. Been long time.*"

My mind races with the possibilities of what is going on. Is this something more than an influencer? How long has this thing been inside its Push?

A slow tug repeats from behind me. Jax and the others are trying to reel me in. I strengthen my mental foundation, not ready to return empty-handed.

"Please, give me back my mother."

The cloud of spinning smoke shrinks and loses its circular form. A haze of dark embers trickles out like feathery strings. A form begins to emerge from the ball of smoke. The dark tendrils form thin lines that transform into a human-looking form. Into... my mother.

I step forward, pushing the limits of the tether holding me in reality. "Mom? Is that you?"

My mother's face emerges from the dark smoke, not fully solid. "Kay, I told you to not come for me."

"I had to. I can't lose you. Where are you?"

Her face goes cold and her eyes turn black. "*She is everywhere. She is here. There.*"

I shake my head, anxiety entangling my inner thoughts. "Why did you take her? What is the point of all this?"

My mother's form evaporates, the spiraling orb of ominous smoke re-emerges. "*Her connection special.*

Navigating time impressive. You're connected awareness special. Both must be awakened. We must be one."

In all my years of using my Push ability, I've never witnessed something like this. I know our collective consciousness is intertwined, but whatever this thing is has gone beyond what I understand our reality to be. My curiosity wants me to learn more, but my rational mind wants me to run.

I calm my inner turmoil and face the ominous presence. "If we are all one, let my mother go and take me. If I join you, doesn't that mean you have everything you need?"

"Understanding is impressive. Incomplete, though. We are one, but each of us controls a plane of reality that is our own. Mother has an individual connection. Your connection different, flexible."

As its final word echoes through my mind, a hole opens in the center of the smoky orb. My mother stumbles out, fully formed. Instantly, her awareness fills my mind, and I know it is her. Knowing the second I connect with her this thing will take me and probably her too, I wrap my arms around her and envelop her essence, bringing her inside me as her form evaporates. As soon as she's with me, I disconnect from my Push, pulling myself along my tether, back to my body that's in reality.

My senses explode as if I can smell and feel everything around me. As if taking my first breath as a newborn baby. My eyes burst open to the familiar outpost walls surrounding me. I topple over off my chair and onto the ground. Lifting my head up, I find Jax, Ava, and the others gaping at me. I jump to my feet, barely able to maintain my stability. Spinning on my heels, I see her. My mother lays on the ground, several feet away from our gathering. My knees buckle, emotions flooding my entire body.

I drop to the ground right in front of her. "Mom?"

Her eyes slowly flutter open. She looks directly at me and a soft smile warms her exhausted face.

I lift my mother up close and pull her into an embrace. Before I can say another word, a heavy thud rattles the structure, dust fluttering down from the ceiling. A loud boom echoes in the distance. The structure shakes again.

Behind me people jump to their feet, trying to figure things out. Farren emerges from the stairwell, into our room. His eyes are wide as he looks from me to my mother. Surprise registers on his face, but fear fills his voice when he speaks.

"The Southern Alliance found us."

CHAPTER TEN

"Caiden and Gareth have got the main entrance!" Farren shouts to Jax as gunfire begins pelting the outer walls. "Erin and Nance are watching the rear exit."

My mom tries to stand up but collapses back onto the floor. I grasp her by the armpits and drag her against the back wall, hoping they don't start firing at us from that direction. Ava and Envee crouch beside us, the younger girls' eyes round with fear. And something like guilt or shame. She was the only Influencer who hadn't been in there searching for my mother, but she lacked the ability to watch our awareness.

"Hey." I grab her hand. "You couldn't have known."

She nods, but her face is hard. Way older than her twelve years. This life has that effect on people. I'm trying to think of what else I could say to reassure her when Stratton drops to his knees in front of me, already reaching for my pistol.

"Can I have this?" he asks.

I look at my weakened mother and know I won't be heading to the front line. "Take it. Go."

Stratton grabs the gun and disappears downstairs just as another boom rattles the building.

When the floor has finished shaking, I stand and look at Farren. "What are we going to do? We're pinned down."

Farren peers out a cracked window, quickly pulling his head back. He checks his handgun and then locks eyes with me. "I don't know. I don't know. We're heavily outnumbered and outgunned."

My chest tightens, and I almost forget to breathe. This is all too familiar. But this time there's more than just me at risk. I'm about to walk over to Farren when my mother puts her hand on my leg, stopping me. I crane my neck to look down at her.

She swallows hard. "You're going to have to save us. There's no other way."

I just stare at her, unable to speak. She knows the only way we get out of this is if I bring on the horde of animals in this forest. Doing that last time was the worst thing I've ever done. The death and carnage were horrifying.

A heavy bang rattles the building once more, jarring me from my thoughts. I turn and the front wall cracks, a jagged line snaking its way to the ceiling. Miya and Amanda rush away from the unstable wall.

This building's not going to last much longer.

Farren darts over to me and grabs my hand. "We've got to take our people and run."

Over my shoulder, I spot Jax standing still with his eyes closed. "There are people scattered throughout the woods. They're everywhere." He opens his eyes and faces Farren and me. "There's no clear path."

I steady my breathing and rest my free hand on Farren's chest. "I'll clear the forest."

Farren drops his shoulders to meet my gaze. "There's got to be another way. I don't want you to go through that again."

I offer him a less than reassuring smile. "I've got this. It's the only way."

Farren doesn't say another word and simply nods, knowing I'm right.

I catch my mother staring at me, her eyes wide with concern now even though it was her idea. She won't try to stop me with so many lives at stake, but I know what she's thinking. What about the thing inside my Push?

Jax sidles up to me. "I'll stay with your awareness and make sure you stay connected to this reality."

Farren pats him on the shoulder. "Thank you."

Ava pulls Envee in close as Jax and I make our way past them to the stairwell. She mouths the words, "I'm sorry."

Envee could extend my reach, allowing me to connect with far more wildlife, but there is no way we're going to allow her to be exposed to that dark presence. She's already terrified. No twelve-year-old should be put through that. I should know.

Farren shadows my movements, following me into the narrow stairwell. Jax trails behind him, ready to watch my mental back.

I tuck my body into the corner of the small landing before the staircase. Jax slides down the wall and sits next to me. Farren readies his weapon and spots up with a clear vantage point down to the bottom level. He nods to me with confidence set in his dark brown eyes. It's going to be hard to focus with the attacks outside, but I take a deep breath and exhale slowly.

It's now or never.

The chaotic sounds of the battle begin to fade as I fall into my awareness. An empty silence emerges; only the steady bond from Jax remains. There's no time to waste and I extend my reach into the greater forest surroundings. Towering shadowy trees sprawl across the murky landscape the further I push out.

Moments later, a small pride of mountain lions consumes my focus. Larger points of light mark their location just over the ridge near this outpost. Shimmering light radiate from the large cats' brilliant silhouettes.

Like a rush of water pouring over a waterfall, I flow into their conscious realities, consuming the entire pride. Four beautiful lions are connected to me, ready for my influence.

I tap into their maternal primal instincts, projecting a sense of urgency to protect displaced cubs near the outpost. These creatures have no choice but to believe my deception is real. I control every aspect of these pure animals. They fight for me and only me now.

Digging deeper into the expanded reach of my Push, I quickly come across two large grizzly bears hunting in the stream about a quarter of a mile from my location. The memory of that large bear stomping on the Vernon Society officer flickers before my mind. I have no choice but to push that guilt away and force my will onto these large predators.

Tapping into their senses, I consume their desires by projecting the memory of the savory feast Jax and I enjoyed at the Vernon Society compound in Seattle. The wild beasts become crazed with hunger, charging toward my delusion.

Retracting from my Push, the surrounding landscape blurs and falls into the darkness. I'm about to return to my body when I spot something in my peripheral. I shift my awareness and notice a young woman with a short, pitch-black, shoulder-length haircut staring right at me, hazel eyes trained hard on me. She wears a leather jacket as she folds her arms across her chest. She's short, but the confidence she carries makes her seem larger than life.

"Everything you do brings connection," a steady female voice cuts through my thoughts. *"You cannot hide or run from me. You tie me to reality. Assistance will be given. Your light must go on."*

My mind spins. Is this the same dark presence? I hold onto the edges of my Push, lingering in this fading awareness.

"What's going on?" I pause for a moment. "Are...are you the one that's been following me in my subconscious?"

This young female form jabs at my curiosity. If this is the same dark presence, she is no longer as intimidating as the ominous black orb of smoke. Confusion fills my inner thoughts.

The girl strides toward me slowly, maintaining eye contact. "You anchor me to this physical plane." No longer does the voice echo throughout my consciousness. She speaks directly to me like a real person. "I never thought I would feel this body again." She caresses the sleeves of her smooth jacket. "Strange, but I've missed it."

I take a step back. "What do you mean you're going to assist me?"

She flits her eyes up slowly before returning them to me, a subtle grin inching up her face. "You and your people are about to die. I'm not done with you. I have more to learn. So, I will help you."

All I want to do is wake up to my current reality and hide from this person, but I can't dismiss what she says about my people dying. "How are you going to help us?"

"Oh, I'm not going to help them, I'm going to help you help them."

A pulsating wave radiates around her, vibrating with each expansion as it pushes toward me. Translucent yet alive with amber shades of light, this ripple expands far beyond anything I've seen from the consciously aware people I've felt before. As if I was in my real-world body, I raise my arms to shield me from the oncoming pulse, but as it reaches me it just phases right through my being and beyond.

I spin and watch as the wave floods the subconscious horizon. A steady hum rumbles all around me.

"What are you doing?" I shout over the deep, thrumming sound.

She answers without moving her lips, and somehow, I process her words in my mind without actually hearing anything. *"The planet is an aware entity just as much as people and wildlife. With the right connection, it can also be persuaded to help."*

I close my eyes tightly as the wave of energy intensifies, tugging at my subconscious form.

And just like that, there's nothing. No rippling wave, no frightening hum—nothing.

Hesitation keeps me from opening my eyes, but the warm air that flows across my face distracts me enough to look. Bright sunlight pulsates down from above, washing over the familiar evergreens of the Cascade mountain range. Somehow it is no longer nighttime and I am back in the current reality. Or am I?

Slowly, I take in a full three-hundred-and-sixty-degree view of our surroundings. There's no outpost or road, just a clearing with tall grass. A dense tree line encircles our location. Floral hints wash across my face as the cool wind swirls.

"Kay?" Farren's voice cuts through the air. "Kay? What the—"

Shaking the fog from my head, I turn to find him emerging from the woods, followed by Ava and Envee. Where is everyone else? Do I even want to know?

I take a few hesitant steps toward him, afraid this is some sort of trick or mirage, but then he is running toward me, closing the gap with desperate speed. Exhausted and disoriented from the Push, I plant my feet and wait. He crashes into me, sliding his strong arms around my waist and spinning me around with... joy?

My stomach churns as my legs pull toward the sky.

"Farren." I cling to his shoulders, burying my face in his neck to hide my eyes from the whirling scenery. "Put me down."

He sets me on my feet, but while the world is still tilting, he cups my face in his hands. A manic grin cuts across his face right before his lips smash against mine. I press my hands into his chest to steady myself, unable to resist his fervor. The kiss is sloppy because I can't quite gain control of my lips, but Farren doesn't seem to mind.

"Huh. I'd almost forgotten what love looks like," the familiar voice dances with the wind. "Kind of... gross."

Farren and I jerk apart and then come back together, clinging to each other's arms as we take in the stranger. Arms crossed and one slender leg jutting out to the side, the girl from my awareness stands in the middle of the clearing, confidence and contempt exuding from her eyes.

CHAPTER ELEVEN

FEAR DIGS ITS CLAWS into my chest, squeezing out all of my air. The girl—the embodiment of the thing that's been stalking me inside my Push—lifts her chin and brows in a smug greeting. No, that's not quite right. Not a greeting. A challenge.

What have I unleashed?

"Who are you?" Farren growls, trying to push me behind him.

I shove his overprotective arm away. "She's—"

"Did I pass out or something?" Amanda blurts from behind me. "I am SO confused right now."

Relief flushes out the fear. For a moment, anyway. Glancing over my shoulder because I can trust that Farren's eyes are locked on the strange girl, I see Amanda and my mother not far behind us. Other figures lurk near the tree line with their weapons drawn. A quick count tells me everyone is here.

"Don't shoot!" I order, throwing out my hands and leveling my gaze on the girl. "She's the reason we're alive!" And then more quietly to myself, I add, "I think…"

Farren's eyes dart between us, wary. "Who…?"

I press my extended hand against Farren's chest and take a step forward. "Is that right? You pulled us out of there?"

But the girl doesn't seem to be listening now. She's staring down at her own body, patting her hands over her arms and thighs with a look of consternation on her face.

"Right?" I ask again, inching closer.

"Huh?" She glances up, dismissive. "Oh, yes. I did that."

Farren's fingers brush my back, urging me not to go any closer. "Who are you?" he demands.

"Um…let me think." She chews on her lip, and then breaks into a smile. "Renee. That's right. My name is Renee."

"Renee?" I repeat, unsure what I was expecting, but certain that wasn't it.

The girl steps forward, extending her hand. "This is how it's done, yes? A handshake? That's how people still meet?"

"Still?" Farren whispers.

"Yes," I reply, stepping forward with my hand out. "I'm—"

"Kay, hold on," my mother's voice cuts through the clearing, full of strength even while her tone remains weak. "I'm coming."

Farren and I both turn toward her. She stands tall with one arm on Amanda's shoulder, trying to play it off as a show of reassurance to one of her soldiers instead of the need for support that it is. Farren—missing the point like the man he is—jobs over to them, offering an elbow.

Mom glares at the jutting limb and pushes past it, holding her head as she strides toward me. Farren hovers right behind her, brows knit with worry. But Leeyah has it under control, even if the beads of sweat on her brow betray the effort this is taking. She stops beside me, resting one hand between my shoulders. I stiffen my spine, trying to give her a steady place to lean.

"I know who you are, and you're not welcome here," Leeyah says firmly. "Leave my daughter alone. Our people do not need you interfering in their lives."

Renee's grin fades, lips forming a fine line. "A mother's Love is very unfamiliar to me. Interesting, but not needed. I'm not your ally nor your enemy. I am all of you. It's time for us to wake up."

"Oh, good," Amanda mutters. "That clears up everything."

"What is this?" Caiden snarls, storming loudly through the grass to join Amanda. "Is this girl a threat or not? I have her in my sights."

Farren raises a fist over his shoulder, steadying Caiden. "Stand down. We don't know what we're dealing with here."

"Kaylin, Leeyah," Jax calls out as he follows the path Caiden stomped into the grass. "Her awareness is everywhere. She surrounds us."

I turn back to Renee who twirls a strand of her jet-black hair as if she's never seen anything so fascinating. Noticing my attention, she tosses the hair over her shoulder and glides toward me, her movements eerily fluid for someone who just got a body. She holds out her hands as if to calm all of us.

"Stay where you are," Farren barks, jumping in front of my mother and me.

Renee obeys but not without sighing loudly. "I see further explanation is required. But first I suggest we retire to somewhere more comfortable." Her teenage attitude mixes with her formal speech pattern in a very unsettling way.

"I think we're good here," I say, grasping Farren's shoulder and scooting him aside. I appreciate his care, but he needs to let me and Leeyah handle this… thing.

Renee rolls her eyes and cocks her head. "Perhaps I should have said somewhere safer. The animals you incited have been hunting all night. It's been a while since I occupied your side of things, but I imagine they have not become vegetarians. We should get inside."

I'd almost forgotten my Push. The mountain lions and bears I unleashed on the Southern Alliance. I swallow hard as my stomach tightens. Scanning over the tree line, I listen for any sounds of commotion. I'm not willing to open my awareness to feel the area with Renee standing just feet from me. My group stirs with uncertainty as they frantically look all around.

"She's right then. We should find shelter," Farren insists as he moves his arm to take my hand, gripping it firmly. "We don't know what's happened since the outpost. We need to get our bearings here."

"At last. Someone who sees reason." Renee smiles sweetly, and though I know it's absurd, I feel a surge of rage. Her gaze drifts away from him and the smile fades. "I'm assuming you'll insist on bringing all of them?"

"We do," my mother answers, waving a hand to indicate our entire group. "This is a package deal."

Renee smirks. "I'm not sure it's a great value, but very well. There's an abandoned hunting lodge just over that ridge." She extends one leg and swivels around as though performing some odd ballet move. "I'm very excited to stretch out these legs. Shall we?"

***

All of us keep a healthy distance from Renee as we follow her up a narrow trail into the wilderness. No one's said much in the last ten minutes. I can feel everyone's uncertainty exuding from their being. It's like a constant itch that tickles the back of my neck. The more I get to know these people, the more their familiar essence intertwines with my conscious reality.

A break in the tree line catches my attention. The midday sun flickers through, forcing me to squint. I raise a hand to shield my eyes and the towering silhouette of a log cabin comes into view. As we approach, more details come in focus. Weathered and splintered, the structure is made of old, thick logs stacked onto each other in an interlocking pattern in the middle of a sloping hillside. Three stories high, this so-called lodge looks more like an old-world military compound than the rustic getaway that I was expecting to find.

"Here we are now," Renee says without turning. "I haven't sensed people here for years. It shouldn't be ransacked. I'm betting you are all hungry?"

How is it that she can know when people were here? Conscious awareness must leave an imprint on an area, but I've never felt this before.

Renee gestures for us to follow as she steps onto a leveled-off dirt road that leads to a wood staircase at the base of the lodge. A rickety, metal overhang juts out next to the stairs. Two rusted small vehicles are parked underneath. They're some sort of busted up all-terrain buggies. Most of the tires are shredded. These things have been sitting here for a long time.

"There's no one inside," I say to the group. "Stay alert, though."

Breathing heavily, Amanda sidles up to me. "Are you sure we should be following this chick? I mean look at her... she looks like an overly edgy Harvester or something."

"Just keep the others ready." I look back at Stratton and Ava who make their way onto the road from the trail. "I don't think our Influencer abilities will do much around her."

Amanda nods and pats me on my back. I refocus on Renee who walks slowly to the staircase, her chin lifted to the sky. She's soaking in the fresh air like she's missed it.

We keep a safe distance from Renee but follow her up the creaky steps. Farren and Caiden lead our people through an open entrance on the first level. As I enter, a cloud of musky dust tickles my senses, making my eyes water a bit and my nose twitch.

Renee finds a leather couch near a large wood stove. She plops down and almost moans at the apparent comfort. She doesn't even pay attention to the rest of us as we funnel in.

"Oh heck yeah," Erin says as she rummages through cabinets in a small kitchen off of the seating area. "There's a crap-ton of canned food in here."

Miya and Nance join her and pull out all the food, placing the cans on the narrow countertops. My empty stomach growls, but Jax and Leeyah intercept me.

My mother furrows her brow as she eyes Renee. "We need to figure out what she is before this goes any further, Kay. People don't just appear out of thin air."

I cast a longing look at the food, but I know she's right. "How though? It's like she only speaks in riddles."

"Maybe we need to ask better questions," Jax says, folding his arms. "Her ability is... it's different. Something more."

"More than what?" I ask, darting a glance at the girl sprawled on the couch. But I already know the answer. I just don't want it to be true.

"Human," Mom says, frowning. "We need to confront her... it... now. All of us Influencers. Well, not Envee."

"Right," I say with a heavy sigh. "Let's do this."

I wave Ava and Stratton over, and then motion to Farren too. He has no Push, but I still want him with me for this. Caiden realizes what we're doing and starts to walk over too, but I step away from the others to cut him off.

"We need to keep this small and intimate," I whisper. "I don't want to spook her and cause problems."

His orange brows furrow. "I'll play nice."

I stand taller and shake my head. "Dude, sorry. This is how it has to go down. Get some food and relax for a minute." I turn and look out the filthy front windows just beyond the sitting area. Shifting back to Caiden, I lock my eyes with his. "We need you and the others watching our backs. We can't scan the greater awareness. You and Nance need to keep this lodge secure."

He huffs and puffs a bit, but eventually nods. "Not sure when you became my boss, but I do trust you. Don't screw this up."

I punch him in the shoulder and he feigns a grimace. He laughs and lifts his hands up, pretending to be intimidated by me. Amanda comes up and grabs his elbow, dragging him to the kitchen. I smile at her and she winks. She's always there when I need her. I take in a deep breath and release it through pursed lips before spinning back to rejoin the others.

"You ready?" Farren asks.

I lift one eyebrow and smirk. "Sure, why not?"

There's a torn-up couch, plus two lumpy lounge chairs directly across from the leather couch that Renee has posted up on. We spread out and form a wall in front of her. Renee pulls her legs off the couch and sits up straight, resting her elbows on her thighs.

She forces a smile only at me. "What's on your mind?"

Stratton scoffs. "How about you tell us who the hell you are?"

Renee glances at him, but her face remains pointed at me. "This feels very aggressive. Perhaps you could all sit down? I just got this body and I'm not in any hurry to damage it, so you needn't worry about an attack."

I look at Farren and then to my mother. She subtly tilts her head as if to say it's my choice, and I feel a surge of pride at how much she's letting me take the lead on this. Maybe it's just because she's still feeling weak from her ordeal, but it still feels like a vote of confidence I didn't even know I needed.

"Fair enough," I say, lowering my palms to indicate that we should all sit.

I sink onto the couch with Farren and Mom. Jax and Ava take the two lounge chairs, leaving Stratton perch on the couch arm beside my mother. Of course.

Renee smiles, gaze still trained on me. As if the others don't really exist. "I'm no different than you. An Influencer, as they call us." She rolls her eyes. "Only more enlightened, if I might put it bluntly."

"We'd actually like you to put it even more bluntly," Stratton says. "Because that clears up... nothing."

"It clears up everything," Renee says simply. "What else do you need to know?"

Ava speaks up, ticking questions off on her fingers. "Let's start with: How did you move us? How is it daytime right now? Were we unconscious? Are we *still* unconscious?"

"All very good questions, but a bit too simple," Renee frowns at me. "Our collective consciousness is far more intertwined than you know. Everything you see, feel, or experience is an illusion we are all working to create."

"You're just throwing words around," Stratton growls, and in my peripheral vision, I see my mother reach over and touch his knee, stilling him.

"We're all Influencers here," Leeyah says. "We all know there's more to this reality than what we're seeing in any given moment, but are you trying to tell us that *none* of this is real?"

Renee finally tears her gaze away from my face, giving my mother an appraising once-over. "Perhaps, but I would need a chalkboard and an overwhelming amount of math to prove it to those operating on your level. It would be easier on your brains to just believe me."

"We're not stupid," I snapped. "But fine, let's come back to that later. What does this being an illusion have to do with how you can move people through space and time?"

"Well, Kaylin," Renee says slowly, as if I were, in fact, very stupid. "If everything is an illusion that includes both space and time, don't you think?"

"And your age?" I ask, narrowing my eyes at her. "That's an illusion too?"

Renee smiles and gives me an approving nod. "Now we're getting somewhere. Yes, my spirit—for lack of a better word—has been around much longer than this body makes it appear." She stretches out her slender arms, rotating them at the elbows and wrists. "I have you to thank for the lack of arthritis."

"Me?" I point at my chest.

"You're the one generating me." She spreads her arms wide. "I am only tethered to this plane by your own abundant awareness."

"Then why can we all see you?" Farren butts in, giving me time to try and wrap my head around what she just said. "Even those of us who have no Push abilities at all?"

Renee's head swivels past me to rest on his face. She adjusts her position on the couch, crossing her fit legs in a manner clearly meant to distract him. Her hand lightly brushes her exposed collarbones as she replies, "We are all connected. We are all capable. Even you. But for me, Kaylin is simply a bit more, shall I say, alluring?"

Farren's eyes bulge out of his head. I reach over and grip his hand to reassure him I'm not about to run off with this cryptic-talking girl who used to be a dark entity that lived inside my Push and kidnapped my mother. She put it like that just to mess with him, I can tell.

Beyond Farren, I notice this level of the house has emptied out. Pyramids of can food take up most of the counters, but Miya and Nance are nowhere to be seen. Same for Caiden, Amanda, Erin, and Envee. Most likely, the ones I didn't send out to secure the perimeter are exploring upstairs, but there's a pinch of uncertainty in my throat. As long as us Influencers are this distracted by Renee, everyone is in danger.

"You don't have to restrain from using your abilities," Renee's words pull me back to our discussion. "But I can tell you that everyone is fine."

My jaw drops open a bit, and I tilt my head to the side. "Can you read my thoughts?"

"Too simple again," Renee says calmly. "The connection we have with each other goes beyond thoughts and words. I simply read the mood of people and understand how behavior can affect reality."

"Well, of course," Stratton huffs, folding his arms and rolling his eyes. "Makes perfect sense."

Renee smiles, missing his sarcasm. "Of course it does."

Ava lifts her hand as though we're in a classroom. "But if you're just like us, then how are you able to use your ability on us when we can't use ours on each other?"

Or on Renee. That's what we're all thinking. We have no real way to stop her except through physical force, and I'm not sure her form is physical enough for that to even work. She might just vanish back into the big illusion or whatever.

Renee stares out the window for a few seconds before facing Ava. "We are not a different species from other humans. We are just tapped into the greater awareness. Most of you so-called Influencers have the ability to guard your minds against each other, but this doesn't mean you are immune to influence. We can play with all aspects of reality. There's more than just our individual minds. Don't you see?"

My cheeks flushed red because I didn't. She was still speaking in riddles, but I hated letting on that I couldn't keep up with her. Was she really saying that Influencers were susceptible to being influenced as much as anyone else? And if that was true, and she had the ability to transport us to another time and place, what else could she do to us?

I lean in close and rest my elbows on my knees. Taking a deep breath, I try to walk it back to a simpler level of questioning. "Okay, so how old are you?"

Renee mimics my posture so that our faces are close together, like we're just two friends sharing secrets. "A lady never reveals her age, Kaylin, but if my math is correct, it's been over fifty years since I was first discovered. So you can infer from that."

"Fifty years ago?" Leeyah asks, touching my wrist to tag herself into the interrogation. "It's only been thirty since I became aware of my own ability, and at the time, everyone spoke as though we were the first wave. You're saying we predate that?"

Renee leans back, pressing her fingertips together. "There's always a patient zero, isn't there?"

My mouth falls open and I automatically reach for Mom's hand. "You were... the first?"

"The first to get caught, anyway." Renee shrugs. "There was no one to tell me how far I could go, and..." A sad look flickers over her features. "I kept pushing the limits of my Push, searching for answers, until eventually, the link broke between me and reality. My consciousness became one with the collective."

"Then how are you still you at all?" I asked softly, feeling a wave of sympathy for her story.

"I'm not," she says. "But then, neither are you. Just because we experience ourselves doesn't many that any of us actually exist."

Stratton jolts to his feet, startling me. "If I don't exist, then who's about to wipe that smug look off your face?"

My mom reaches out and grabs his arm, jerking him into the small space left beside her on the couch. "Quiet."

Renee laughs. "I like you, tough guy. You aren't as serious as the others. Think of reality as a computer simulation. Everything can be manipulated if you understand the code. Somehow, some of us became intertwined in the universe's code, giving birth to the enlightened."

"Who *exist*," Stratton growls, thumping his chest. "I'm here. I'm breathing. Are you?" He narrows his eyes.

She smiles enigmatically. "I can if you want me to."

Stratton clamps his hands over his head, and I feel like she may be giving him a dose of his own medicine. He definitely seems ready to jump off a cliff.

I raise a hand grabbing Renee's attention. "Okay, okay, can we slow down on the metaphysics? Practically speaking, how did you bring us all here?"

"I didn't bring you anywhere," Renee says, leaning back and spreading her arms over the couch cushions. "Like your mother, I just slipped us out of their current moment by slowing how your enemies perceive time. Then I neutered your connection to reality. In a sense, you became a mindless herd that followed me to where you woke up many hours later. That sort of manipulation requires me to break you away from your connection to our physical planet." She pauses for a moment, trying to gather words that make this sound less crazy. "Everything in the universe is made of the same elements and particles. The moment you become consciously aware of your existence you become linked to that world. Sort of like how birds cling to their nest for so long. Again, everything is connected."

Farren leans forward, his face twisted with confusion. "Being around so many Influencers I've seen a ton of weird stuff, but what you are saying is beyond what I can understand. I'm not even sure I want to try. All I really care about is if you are a threat to us or not."

Renee slowly stands and walks over to the sprawling window and stares out into the expansive forested horizon. "I was lost for decades, but your friend here brought me back. I didn't mean to alarm any of you with my actions. Being stuck inside the subconscious realm disconnects you from humanity. I was just trying to find something to latch onto."

"So why this illusion still?" My mother points up and down the girls' lithe, young body. "Why not show us your true self?"

Renee looks over her shoulder but doesn't turn. "Perception is reality. I'm not that old woman anymore. Why would I want to go back to that? Our spirits are neither young nor old. Our physical bodies determine when we stop experiencing this particular simulation of existence. I'm not done here."

I push off from Farren's knee and stand. Walking over to Renee, I look deep into her eyes. "Okay, then what's next?"

Intensity burns in her gaze. "It's time to wake up the world."

CHAPTER TWELVE

"Well that doesn't sound ominous or anything," Stratton blurts from the sitting area.

I quickly look over my shoulder and glare at him before turning back to Renee. "Yeah, uh, what do you mean by wake up the world?"

Renee adjusts her jacket and spins on her heels. I follow her as she moves in front of the leather couch, scanning over those sitting on the couch and chairs. She ruffles her hair. "I've gone through decades of Humanity's worst atrocities. It is not a coincidence that Influencers have emerged. Like with all great transitions, there's going to be friction and abuse." She paces the small area between the couches. "The ebbs and flows of consciousness are not random. My awareness intersecting with Kaylin was a sign. This reality has reached the tipping point. It is time for it to be pushed in the right direction."

My mom swiftly stands and steps up next to me. "Hold on there. I get that you've been around for a while, and maybe you have a larger perspective than the rest of us, but this sounds like some sort of... genocide of reality. What are you saying?"

Renee takes in a tempered breath and turns to face us, blowing the air out evenly. "I'm saying you have collected the perfect assortment of abilities and with my help, we can change this world and make it something better."

I shake my head. "Manipulating the minds of those who want to hurt and control others is one thing, but this sounds like you want to push everyone, and who's to say you know the right direction?"

Renee's eyes narrow into dark slits. She says nothing, but within moments I hear the sound of boots on the stairs. Miya and Amanda come trotting down, expressions serene. The front door opens and more people file in, led by Caiden and Nance, all of their faces eerily calm.

"What are you doing?" I demand, glaring at Renee. "Stop this."

The rest of the Influencers scramble to their feet. I press against my mother's side, and her arm closes over my shoulders. As if drawn to her anxiety, Stratton crosses to her other side. He waves an angry hand in front of Renee's face, but she ignores him.

"Jax," I say, searching out my cousin's steady gaze.

As our eyes meet, his features seem to flicker and then slacken with resignation. Then the same thing happens to Ava. Mom's hand clamps on my upper arm, holding me to her. Motion catches our attention across the room, and we both turn to see Envee nudging through the line of non-Influencers to come stand blandly by Ava's side.

"That's enough," my mother says quietly. "We get the idea."

Renee smiles. "No, I don't think you do."

Farren, the last person sitting, suddenly vaults to his feet. Instinctively, I reach for his hand, yearning to draw him close, but he doesn't even look at it. He stares straight ahead, eyes racing back and forth. There's a pull on my chest, stuttering my breath. That's impossible.

"Farren?" I ask, trying to quell the tremble in my tone. "What are you doing?"

His head turns slowly. Almost robotically. "Sorry, Kay, she's right. Things can't go on like this anymore. People need to be woken up."

My heart drops into my stomach, tears welling in my eyes. She has him.

"What are you doing to them?" I plead to Renee. "How are you affecting him?" I point at Farren. "He has the implant. He can't be Pushed."

Renee moves closer to my mother, Stratton, and me. She slips an arm around Farren's waist and pats him on the chest. "How many times do I have to tell you? Consciousness cannot bound by human trinkets. There are no limitations."

I look desperately between Jax and Ava, but they are nodding in agreement. Anger settles in my stomach. At Renee, for doing this. At myself, for unleashing her. At Billy Wilson, for finding us back at the outpost. At the

Southern Alliance. At my aunt and uncle. At everyone who has ever hated us or tried to use us as tools to hate others.

"You can't do this," I snarl, fists bunching at my sides. "Jax. Ava. Snap out of this. Envee. Come on."

Ava lifts her chin slowly and glances at Jax before meeting my glare. "I'm sorry, Kay, but... I'm tired of being hunted like a rabid dog. And I don't want this life for her." She takes Envee's hand. "Renee has the power to make real change. I'm tired. I don't want to keep fighting."

I gape at her, an uneasy feeling gathering in my stomach. Farren spoke as though he were a puppet, but Ava seems entirely present. My eyes flash to Jax, who ducks his head and stares at the ground. My rage turns into a pounding sensation in my head. I want a different life just as much as anyone, but what Renee was suggesting... He couldn't possibly be considering it.

"Jax, I know things have been rough, but you can't let her get to you. You've got to fight her off." I glare at Renee. "Let them go!"

Jax sighs and runs a tired hand through his hair. "She's not manipulating us, Kay. Ava and I have been struggling with our place in this world for a while. Maybe it's time we try something different. Maybe it's time to use our abilities to fix this broken planet."

My mouth drops open, words refusing to come out. Farren's words hurt because I know he is being controlled, but Jax is choosing this. He honestly believes we should let Renee push the world in the right direction without even asking what that direction might be. Maybe I am a pessimist, but as bad as things are, I can still see plenty of ways in which they can be worse.

Renee steps toward me, ignoring the hand my mother holds up to warn her away. "Kaylin, you are part of this. We need you by our side. I know there's a part of you that believes I'm right. Together, we can set everyone on the right path to a better future."

Emotions force me to swallow hard. "You're wrong. A person's awareness is not something that anyone has the right to manipulate. There's a difference between using our abilities to fight for freedom and using them to play God or whatever it is you want to do."

Renee looks at me with pity. "So much talent, yet your mind remains so small. Have you been listening to me? Everything is an illusion. Right now, it's a nightmare, but we have the ability to turn it into a dream. You would deny all those who are suffering because of your own self-righteousness?"

Mom pushes me behind her and steps up to Renee. "I may not be as old as you, but I'm old enough to know that these promises never come true. This isn't about the world; it's about you. It makes me wonder if you really got lost in your awareness, or if the awareness knew it wasn't safe to let you out. Surely in fifty years you could have found someone before my daughter."

"The collective consciousness is larger than anything you have ever imagined," Renee says. "One could wander for decades without coming across another soul. But there were others, yes. None of them with enough power to bring me through."

"I won't let you use her like this," Mom snarls, and then points at Jax. "And you. You're too smart to be falling for this."

Jax shuffles his feet. "I understand there are risks, Leeyah, but we can't keep pretending this is a war we can win. Look at us." He motions at our ragtag group. "We're done for. Every day is just another chance to watch someone die."

"Listen to your nephew," Renee says, and a chill works its way down my spine. We've never said anything about our family ties out loud since she arrived. "Do you want to be part of the solution or part of the problem?"

"Okay, nope, I'm done with this crap," Stratton snarls and lunges forward, whipping Farren's pistol out of its holster and spinning it toward Renee. "Go back where you came from."

In unison, Caiden, Nance, Erin, and the other armed members of our group jump into action and train their weapons on Stratton with my mother and me caught in the potential crossfire.

Startled by the synchronized reaction, Stratton raises the weapon and both hands into the air. His eyes widen as he freezes in place. Farren yanks back his weapon and rams the muzzle against the back of Stratton's head.

"Farren!" I shout, tears stinging my eyes, but he doesn't even blink.

"It appears you three are unwilling to join our cause. Am I correct?" Renee asks, shifting her attention between my mother, Stratton and me. "I warn you. One way or the other, you will be a part of this change. You're not strong enough to get in my way."

I wipe the tears from my face as fury consumes my fear. Heat flashes over my entire body. I won't let this happen. Shutting my eyes, I settle my anger, holding it at bay as I focus on my Push. Before I can step out of reality and into my mind's awareness, the air is pulled from my lungs.

My eyes pop open to a completely different setting. On the fringe of my vision, bodies blur as if they've been smeared across a canvas. Amongst the haze of color, a fully in focus Ava and Jax stand just feet from me, their brows furrowed in confusion. I reach for my mother, but she's no longer holding me.

Spinning around, my eyes lock with Renee's in the same moment that my mother's body collides with hers. The girls' eyes fly open in shock as Mom pins her arms to her side and slams her onto the ground.

"Mom!" I shout.

"Kay, go!" She screams. "Now!"

No, not again.

I explode into action, lunging toward my mother, but Stratton cuts me off, wrapping his arm around my shoulders. He mouths "sorry" an instant before an intense thud knocks my head back. White light floods my vision and then everything goes dark.

CHAPTER THIRTEEN

I CLUTCH AT the back of my neck as it throbs with intense pain. This ache floods down from the crown of my head to the middle of my back. My eyelids are heavy, but I will them to open. A cloudy, unfocused form hovers over me. I blink over and over until the haziness solidifies. Stratton leans over me, an awkward smirk plastered on his face.

"Don't kill me," he says, both hands raised.

Slowly, I sit up, planting my hands behind me on the damp grass as the blades reach up through my fingers. As if waking from a deep slumber, my mind is slow to process what's happening around me. I shift my attention from Stratton to my surroundings. Nearly surrounded by bushy ferns, I realize we are still deep in the woods. That's when I remember what happened.

"Did you knock me out?" My words come out as sharp as a knife. "What the hell did you do?"

Stratton scoots back on his knees, giving him a few feet of safety from me. "There was no other way. I knew you wouldn't leave your mom and the others behind. I took advantage of the chaos."

My mind races as I replay what happened at the hunter's lodge. My friends acting like mindless zombies, Ava and Jax avoiding my eyes, and my mother lunging at Renee. I shake my head trying to rattle some sense into my mind.

I slide back and lean on the rough tree trunk that Stratton apparently propped me up on. A wash of sadness encircles my entire body, leaving me numb.

Stratton is right. I would have never left anyone behind, and I probably would have been killed by my own manipulated friends. Everything inside of me wants to punch him in the face and run like a headless chicken back to the lodge, but logic is winning out. I can't fault him for his quick thinking.

I swallow hard and meet Stratton's gaze. "You did the right thing." I gently tap on the growing bump on the back of my head. "But did you have to hit me so hard?"

"Sorry 'bout that." He shrugs his shoulders.

"How long have I been out?"

Stratton's deep brown eyes scan over the forest before returning to me. "About thirty minutes. I've been lugging you through these woods for about a mile. No one's following us."

Without warning my chest tightens and sadness consumes my thoughts. I can no longer hold back the tears as they stream down my cheeks. Amanda, Farren, my mother—everyone is gone.

Stratton hesitates, but eventually plops down next to me. He wraps his arm around my shoulders. Without thinking, I bury my face into his chest and release all the built-up emotions from the day. He rubs my shoulder and says nothing.

A minute passes and all my emotions are drained. I lift my head up and flit my eyes to Stratton before turning to look out on the darkening forest. "Thanks for... well, you know."

Stratton removes his arm and clears his throat as he jumps to his feet. "Yeah, uh, well, you're my people now. We need to stick together."

I take in a deep breath and collect myself. Stratton offers me a hand and I take it as I pull myself up. Drawing my arms in close, I rub the goosebumps away. The air is becoming chilly as evening approaches. Stratton notices and paces around, looking for somewhere to go. He's not wearing a jacket and his exposed forearms show signs of him being cold too. I've never noticed how filled out he is before. I can't help but look at his well-defined muscles. I shake away the senseless thoughts and refocus on our next steps.

"Did you pass by any signs of civilization?" I ask.

He shakes his head. "I didn't really pay attention. You're not the lightest thing in the world to drag around. I was just trying not to collapse."

Somehow, a light chuckle escapes from me. "What direction did we come from?"

Stratton points behind me.

I wave for him to follow me and start the trek back in the direction of the lodge.

He follows but hops in front of me as soon as he catches up. "Whoa, wait. What's the plan here, princess?"

Nearly running into him, I stumble and straighten up. "We've got to head back. Need to find somewhere to keep an eye on things."

"Won't Renee see us coming a mile away?" he asks.

I bite my lip and narrow my eyes, considering all I know about her. Most Influencers only have one special talent, and hers would appear to be disconnecting people from reality and moving them around like pieces on a chessboard. "My instinct is no," I say at last.

"What about through your dreams or whatever?" He asks, brows furrowed. "Didn't she find you there?"

My mind continues to race as I run through everything from the past couple of days. The only place it seemed she truly had the power to find me was inside the greater awareness. My headache grows as I try to figure things out.

"I don't know," I say. "Maybe she can tap into the awareness of my subconscious while I dream. Maybe I opened up to her somehow. But something inside me is telling me that she can't track me in my normal awake state."

Stratton pulls out the pistol he must have stolen back from Farren in those last few seconds, and I instantly flinch at the thought of him hitting me with it. He checks the ammo clip and then holsters it in the back of his pants.

He takes in a deep breath and exhales quickly. "Well, I hope you're right. But we need to figure out how we can use our abilities without her getting to us. I don't like being normal and helpless. What's your plan, boss?"

I take a step away from him and pace a few feet. As if a light bulb flickers on, an idea pops into my head. "I think we need a distraction. Let's send some of Billy Wilson's gang their way."

Stratton scoffs and raises his eyebrows. "Okay, I'm all for doing dumb things and seeing how it works out, but doesn't that seem like it's going to get people killed?"

I shake my head, pacing faster now. "We just need enough time to get in there and get rid of Renee. We'll just send a few. Enough that we can handle when we get our friends back."

Stratton scratches the side of his head, skepticism plain on his face. "I don't know…"

"Do you have any other ideas?" I ask, voice screeching. My mom is in that lodge. Farren and Amanda. Everyone I care about. Everyone that's kept me fighting all this time. "We can't just leave them to her."

Stratton sighs. "Okay, okay, but how do you use your Push if that *magical* witch is watching?"

Crossing my arms across my chest, I grin at Stratton. "I'm not going to... You are."

He tilts his head. "Uhhhh, riiiight. So, what happens when she swallows my soul or whatever inside there?"

"She's not watching for you. She's linked to me and my family." I rest a hand on his shoulder. "She's only been able to find us when either my mom or me used our Push.

It's like my bloodline is tethering her to reality. She couldn't detect you guys when you were using your abilities to give me a lifeline when I got my mom back."

My mind races with possibilities. I'm not sure about any of this, but Stratton must use his abilities, or we are lost. He's all I've got right now.

Stratton steps back as I pull my hand from him. He slowly spins, evaluating our surroundings. "Well, we'll need to get lucky. Not all of them are implant free. This is not going to be easy."

"I'll take whatever we get," I say. "You in?"

He locks his eyes on me. "Alright, I'm in, but no more child locks. I'm gonna do what I gotta do. It might not be pretty."

I avoid thinking about the horror his ability can bring. Instead, I shift my thoughts to my mom, Farren, Amanda, and the others. My chest once again tightens. I need them back.

We jump into action, me scouting out the woods the old-fashioned way as Stratton opens his awareness. He has nowhere near the reach I have, but like any Influencer, he can blanket an area to find people. With no established trails in this area, we have no choice but to climb through thorny vegetation and around immovable boulders. At least, the throbbing pain from Stratton's blow has eased a bit, making it easier to navigate the uneven terrain.

Thirty minutes pass and the desperation is making my lungs stick to my ribs. I can barely catch my breath and a sharp pain forms in my side. Leaning against a tree, I open my mouth to suggest that I take the risk and join in the mental search.

"Got 'em!" Stratton crows before I can. "Over that ridgeline." He stretches an arm out and points two fingers toward a craggy hilltop about thirty yards out. He lowers his voice. "I think there are five of them. Three are implant free."

Closing my eyes, I let myself feel a moment of relief. "Okay, that's good. Can you Push them to flee toward the lodge? We'll have to hurry before the other two call in the whole mob. We don't want more than we can handle."

"You bet, let's do this," Stratton says, taking a few steps toward the ridge.

He closes his eyes, and I watch as his chest rises and falls at an even, slow rhythm. While I wait, I look over my shoulder, worried to see a mob of Renee's making. What will I do if we have to fight our own people? What's even the point of trying to save them then?

"Done," Stratton says as he meets my eyes.

I raise an eyebrow. "Wow, that's quick. What did you do?"

An exaggerated grin spreads across his face. "Let's just say they're not feeling very happy-go-lucky right about now. The only way to remove the heaviness I planted in them is to head the direction I pointed them to."

I shudder, unable to believe things have gotten to the point that I'm encouraging Stratton to use his horrifying talent on anyone, even our worst enemies. He suddenly grabs my wrist and pushes me behind an outcropping of pine saplings. Dropping to one knee, he pulls me next to him and points through a narrow opening between the young trees. I squint to sharpen my focus as three men emerge over the ridge and frantically charge through the overgrown forest floor.

About a half-minute later, another man and woman breach the ledge. They stop to catch their breath as the woman reaches for her handheld radio. We won't have long to take out Renee and get our friends back on our side. The man and the woman half-run, half-stumble down the steep incline and disappear after their miserable companions.

"We should move." Stratton tugs on my arm.

I nod and rise to a crouch. "Keep low. Who knows how many will be coming behind us?"

We follow a narrow creek to mask our heavy footsteps as we run parallel to the manipulated fighters heading toward the lodge. Several exhausting minutes later, we come to an abrupt stop and hunch over to gather our breath. Just up ahead is the dirt road that leads back to the hunter's lodge. All is quiet. Maybe our distractions were struggling to get through the dense forest.

Several rapid pops up ahead make me flinch.

Gunfire.

I lock eyes with Stratton.

He swallows hard and says, "That's probably our guys firing on them."

"If one side is firing, they both are. Let's go. If you get a clear shot on Renee..." I squeeze my eyes shut. "Take it."

Stratton nods, but then hesitates. "What if that doesn't break her hold?"

I glance in the direction of the gunfire, adrenaline buzzing in my brain, making it hard to think. Those bullets could be tearing through the flesh of someone I love. "We'll cross that bridge if we get there. Come on."

I take only one step toward the dirt road before I hear several clicks behind us. Stratton and I spin around and all that adrenaline flies out of me as my heart sinks in my chest.

Billy Wilson and about a half-dozen, heavily armed men stand between the trees, their weapons trained on us.

Billy Wilson narrows his dirt-brown eyes on me. "Do you really think we're going to fall for that crap again?"

CHAPTER FOURTEEN

STRATTON AND I lift our arms. He lets his pistol fall to the ground, and I can't stop my tears from joining it. They slide down my cheeks and drip off my chin. Billy grins, licking his lips at the prospect of finally finishing me off.

"Billy," I say, my voice barely more than a whisper. "Listen to me. There's something in that lodge that threatens all of us. We can work together—"

Billy throws back his head and laughs. If he were alone, it would be the perfect chance to punch him in the throat and escape. But no such luck. His laughter cuts off and he looms closer, flanked by two of his meanest looking grunts.

"We don't work with freaks," Billy spits the words between his yellow teeth. "We kill them."

Billy takes one long stride forward and his gun is jammed against my forehead. This is it. This is how it ends. Everything we've been through, everything we've done... it's all over. Closing my eyes, I consider the possibility that he's got the right idea. Maybe the world will calm down once all the Influencers are gone. Maybe innocent people like Farren and Amanda can go back to living normal lives. And as for those who can Push... well, at least we won't be running.

"Um... Kay?" Stratton's voice breaks the eerie silence that has fallen over the woods.

My eyes flutter open. The cold circle of steel still digs into my face, but the man attached to it has frozen. I take a careful step back and he doesn't blink. My eyes scan the rest of his group and find only human statues.

"Mom?" Hope cracks my voice as I spin on my heels and search for my mother.

But she's nowhere in sight. How...?

Turning back, I see Stratton lean into Billy's distorted face, analyzing every inch. One eye is wide, his lip curled up and his tongue slightly sticking out. Not the most flattering moment to be frozen in. Stratton fiddles with his belt and pulls out a small pocketknife. He grips the handle tightly as his knuckles turn white. He raises the blade up to Billy's throat.

"Whoa, stop!" I plead, reaching out for Stratton. "You can't do that. It's not right."

Stratton cranes his neck and glares over his shoulder at me. "Why the hell not? He deserves it. This punk will not stop until you are dead. This Push has given us the perfect opportunity to eliminate this threat once and for all."

Hand extended, I inch toward Stratton and gently rest my hand on his forearm. "Please. Killing in the heat of battle is one thing, but slicing the neck of someone who's helpless, like this, is not right. I don't care who it is."

He shakes his head and sighs as he slowly pulls the knife from Billy's neck. "You're going to regret this... We're all going to regret this."

My breathing relaxes a bit as I pull my hand back from Stratton. "Thank you."

He shrugs and turns back to Billy. "Now what? This is your mom's doing, right? Where is she? Does this mean Renee knows we're here too?"

"I'm not sure, but we need to rethink this."

"Well, at least we get to up our game," he says as he scans over the stuck-in-time group. He walks past Billy and steps in front of a burly guy in the back. He gently unlatches the strap on his assault rifle and pulls it out of his hands.

I catch on to what he's doing and join him, taking weapon after weapon from Billy's people. We gather a couple of packs and strip them clean of all their weapons and gear. Whatever we can't carry we stash in the thorny brush, deeper into the woods.

Gunfire continues to ring out up by the lodge.

"We've got to get up there," I say. "If Mom gets hit—"

Stratton nods and grabs my shoulder. Together, we scurry up the road, keeping low behind the sloped bank on the side nearest the lodge. After a few minutes, the road angles off and we make the sharp turn to the right. The lodge looms into view.

"There," Stratton whispers as he jerks his chin at the overhanging structure where the busted-up quads sit. I follow his eyes and spot Caiden and Gareth guarding the entrance at the top of the stairs.

Near the bottom of the stairs, three bodies lay covered in blood. It's the fighters we sent at them. Guilt washes over me, which is silly. What did I think was going to happen?

I lead Stratton over to a thick, red cedar tree adjacent to the structure. Neither Caiden nor Gareth change their patrolling pattern. For now, Renee hasn't turned them on us. Hopefully that means she's not aware of our presence.

"How are we going to get in there?" I ask Stratton.

He gnaws on his lower lip for a moment. "Let's use these fun toys we just stole," he says as he digs through the camouflaged pack he brought with us. "Ah, there we go," he says as he pulls out something round.

My eyes go wide as I recognize the grenade in his hand. "Are you crazy? We'll kill our own team!"

He purses his lips and gives me a disappointed glare. "Seriously? I'm not dumb." He pulls out a second grenade from his pack. "We're going to light up this forest and draw them all out."

A slow smile spreads across my face. That Billy Wilson thing turned out alright. As long as they stay frozen.

"Alright, let's do this." I dig in my own stolen pack and grab a grenade. "Let's detonate them about thirty yards apart. You set off the first one over there." I point past Stratton and off to the side of the lodge. "I need

Caiden and Gareth distracted so I can blow up some trees without getting shot."

"But the trees?" He plasters a fake pout on his face. "You're mean."

I grin and shake my head. "Well, you know me, I'll probably plant some new ones because of the guilt." I scan the area for any other signs of our people. I really don't want to blow anyone I care about up. But the area seems clear. Turning back to Stratton, I nod confidently. "You ready?"

"Yep. After the fourth explosion meet me back at the entrance. If we're lucky, Renee will come outside, but more likely we'll have to go in after everyone else runs out."

I swallow hard. "Try your best not to hit anyone else."

He smiles. "Sounds like a plan."

Stratton takes one last glance at the lodge before shuffling off, keeping low behind the overgrown brush. As I wait for the first explosion, my heart pounds like a massive earthquake is rippling through my chest. I try to steady my breathing, but my lungs are burning too much. They might as well be full of smoke.

This is taking too long. Something must be wrong.

Going against everything I know is right, I've just started after Stratton when a dense boom rattles the trees, forcing me to cover my head as sticks and leaves rain down. That's my signal.

Move Kaylin.

I bounce up as if my legs have a mind of their own and bolt in the opposite direction of the explosion. With both grenades in my hands and my assault rifle strapped on my back, I trample through the forest.

After a few seconds, I stop and trigger the first grenade to detonate in ten seconds. I drop it and run, nearly tripping over every log and rock in my way.

Boom.

Birds burst from the trees above, flying in all different directions in a search for safety. I inhale deeply and steady my resolve. I rush to my next spot as another crackling explosion echoes off in the distance. Stratton's other grenade.

Leaning against an outcropping of granite, I set my second grenade and toss it into a shallow creek bed. This time I stay where I'm at and cover my ears.

On cue, the grenade explodes, spraying water and pebbles over my wall of protection.

There's no time to settle my nerves. I pull the heavy rifle from over my shoulder and click the safety off. I tighten the straps on my pack with my free hand and then move. Ducking in and out of my cover, I don't spot anyone and start to run.

Cutting back and forth through the vegetation, I reach the dirt road and find Stratton planted against the side of the lodge with his weapon pointed at the entrance. Caiden and Gareth are nowhere to be seen. Nobody is actually. Our vision of our friends running outside so we could slip in without hurting anyone shrivels and dies like the trees we've just senselessly set on fire.

Keeping low, I stick to the tree line just off the road. Stratton notices me and waves me over. I barely avoid falling as I sprint to him and throw myself against the wall beside him. My lungs burn more than ever, filling with floating ash from the ruined forest.

"I haven't seen anyone," Stratton whispers as he looks over his shoulder at me.

I stretch my neck up to try to get a better view of the entrance above us. Turning back to Stratton, I narrow my eyes. "We have no other choice. We've got to go in."

He drops his shoulders back against the wall and faces me. "So what's the plan if our people start shooting at us?"

A heaviness rolls down my chest, settling in my stomach. I stare at Stratton for a moment. "This is bigger than all of us now. We just have to *try* not to kill anyone."

He raises one brow and purses his lips. "Yeah, um, I know you won't be shooting Amanda or Farren. And I'm not even sure I could shoot your mom if she's nabbed her now."

The emotion in his voice is thicker than I ever thought possible, and I feel ashamed of the jealousy I've been feeling. If anyone ever needed a mother, it's Stratton. And of course, he's right. I'll die before I hurt someone I love. This whole plan was an epic mistake. I should have slowed down, thought bigger as Renee might say. I grip Stratton's wrist and look into his pained eyes. "I got you into this, so I need to do what's right here. I've got to use my abilities to see what's going on in there. I can't hide from her any longer."

"That's not what I meant," Stratton says, clasping his hand over mine. "Let me do some manly stuff and get in there and see what's going on." He smirks. "If I don't come out in a few minutes, then wait a few more, and then get some distance from this place. You're the only one that can match up with Renee if it comes down to that."

I pull away, shaking my head and glaring at him. "No, I'm not going to let you do that."

But before I can do anything, a smattering of voices trickles through the smoky tree line surrounding us.

Stratton grabs his weapon and aims the barrel toward the woods. "I think our frozen friends have thawed."

Adrenaline pumps through my veins, forcing my heart to race. I look back and forth between the lodge and the hazy tree line. What does this mean for my mother? If Renee has hurt her…

"We need to take cover," I say reluctantly. "This is a disaster."

Stratton nods and leads us away from the oncoming danger. Just off of the lodge, we find a slope with a natural alcove under a towering redwood's massive roots. We slide down and tuck ourselves under.

Voices murmur all around us, too far away to understand, but close enough for fear to lock me in place. Stratton and I squeeze into the small opening. Strands of roots dangle from above our heads. We sit on damp soil, and I feel the grainy compost slipping between my fingers as I dig my hands into the dirt.

"Over here," a woman calls in the distance.

My heart thuds so loud that I fear it will give our location away. Glancing at Stratton, I see his intense gaze is trained just at the opening of our little rabbit hole. His rifle's held close to his body, ready to fire at anything that comes. I tighten the grip on my weapon and adjust my pack so I can nestle deeper into this alcove.

A scream echoes through the woods behind us, startling me. The panicked terror gets louder and louder. I pull my legs in tight to my body. Dirt trickles down from above, and then a blur zips over our opening and a woman lands just feet from us. In unison, Stratton and I train our weapons on her, but she doesn't turn and instead sprints deeper into the woods. She grips her head and flails her body wildly.

I've seen this before. It's Ava's Push.

The woman disappears into the darkening woods as evening approaches fast. Several more people scream in terror. Gunshots pop from all around us. It's a war zone. Our people are fighting back, but unless there's been a miracle, they are fighting for Renee. And she won't hesitate to sacrifice them if it keeps her alive. Or whatever she is.

"We can't stay here," Stratton urges.

He's right. We put ourselves right in between the worst of both sides. Renee wants nothing more than to neuter humanity, while Billy wants to eliminate all Influencers.

I look up at Stratton, my last remaining ally. "You go. Save yourself." I swallow hard, emotion and nerves blending together. "Please, go. It's alright. But I can't live if everyone I love is dead. My fate is right here... in this forest. You have a chance to start over. Take it."

Stratton pauses for a moment and then shakes his head. "I told you, princess, you are *my* people. This *is* my second chance. I'm not going anywhere. Let's go be stupid together."

CHAPTER FIFTEEN

BETWEEN THE CONSTANT screams and gunfire zipping through this forest, I'm having the hardest time focusing on my Push. It doesn't help that I'm terrified Renee will step into my awareness.

Stratton is still vigilantly at my side, keeping an eye out for anyone who might stumble across our hiding spot. We can't both use our Push at the same time or we'll leave ourselves vulnerable.

I muffle the overbearing noise with the palms of my hands on my ears, dulling the chaos a bit. A wash of warmth floods over my body as I enter the subconscious state. No longer do I hear the frantic noises that surround my real-world body. I need to do this quick. Absorbing the hazy conscious plane, I analyze as far as I can—as quickly as I can. Constant shadows phase in and out as I observe the battle in the forest. I'm hunting for the vast ripples that consciously aware people exude.

Within seconds, I locate a pack of overlapping waves of awareness. It's our people. The pulsating warmth radiates outward as it intersects with the other people who are tapped into the greater consciousness of this world.

Skimming over the broader horizon like an eagle flying low, I'm searching for a specific ripple. Distance in the subconscious realm is not represented the same as in reality. Everything is spread out across a great expanse in my mind. At the edge of my reach, I feel a familiar warmth and love that I would never forget—Amanda. She is the most consciously aware person I know. Being around me so long has exposed her to a greater understanding of this existence. Only Influencers have an awareness radius greater than hers. She has always been a beacon for me.

There's no time to recruit animals to our cause. Besides, this forest is chaotic enough. I don't think I could deal with anything more. Not wanting to expose myself inside the greater awareness any longer than I have to, I jolt out of my Push and back to my current reality.

"There you are," Stratton whispers. "Five people have almost spotted us. But I guess they're too preoccupied to see what's right in front of them." He quickly leans forward before shifting back to look at me. "Did you find them?"

I blink hard several times, trying to refocus. "Yes. They're together, but not at the lodge. They've taken position near the far ridgeline behind the structure."

"Smart," Stratton says. "I'm sure Caiden came up with that idea. Keep the Southern Alliance preoccupied at the lodge while they do their damage from a distance." He narrows his brow. "Did she see you in there?"

"I don't think so. I didn't feel her."

Stratton lifts an eyebrow. "Okay, perfect. Let's move on them now. If we're going to bring any of them back, this is our best chance."

I simply nod. We adjust our packs and check our ammo. Peeking my head out the alcove, I don't see anyone coming. The surrounding woods are still smoky from our explosions. Cracks and gunfire rattle off all around us as people shout and scream from all directions. I swallow what little moisture I have and lead the way. Stratton follows closely behind as we jump from tree to tree, avoiding any open ground.

Just as Stratton hops over a narrow creek, someone lunges right at him, sending him to the ground. Stratton's rifle and pack fly away from him. A burly man with a thick beard and the standard-issue military attire from the Southern Alliance grits his teeth as he locks his massive forearm around Stratton's neck. They tussle on the ground, fighting for an advantage.

Only a few yards back, I train the barrel of my rifle at the man, but there's no clear shot as they keep rolling around like wild animals fighting to the death.

My heart beats hard and my breath struggles to keep my lungs from burning. I adjust my position over and over again, but I have no shot.

I'm about to drop my weapon and charge over there to jump on the man when the Alliance fighter's eyes go wide and his mouth falls open. The grizzly man releases his death grip on Stratton's neck as his arms fall back and his body goes limp. Stratton rolls over and pulls a blade from the man's gut, blood spurting out onto Stratton's shirt.

Quickly, I re-evaluate our surroundings to make sure there are no more surprises coming before I turn back to Stratton who's breathing hard as he hunches over on the ground. I hop over the narrow creek and drop to one knee next to him. "Are you okay?"

He wipes the sweat from his glistening forehead and meets my eyes. "Yeah... yeah, I think so."

I take one more look at the dead man on the ground next to us before I stand up and offer Stratton a hand. He takes my wrist and I pull him up. He's breathing heavy, but he seems to be alright.

"We have to keep going," I insist. "We're sitting ducks here."

He simply nods and picks up his rifle and pack. We slip into the woods and continue, navigating extra cautious this time.

As we move forward, I analyze Stratton. I would've never imagined he would turn out to be who he is now. He's done a complete one-eighty. He truly cares for me and our people and he's putting his life on the line for us at every turn. It shows that there's still goodness in this world if there's enough love and care to help bring it out.

Soon, darkness blankets the forest, but we're still able to navigate through the overgrowth of vegetation. The constant bursts of gunfire in the distance brighten the area just enough to help guide our way. It seems like Renee keeps moving just beyond our reach.

A sudden warmth floods my core and I grab Stratton's shoulder, stopping him in place. I narrow my eyes as I scour the tree line. "They're up ahead. I can feel them." I whisper.

Cracks of gunfire dull the closer we get to our people. Soft pops echo from behind, shouts and screams fade. It feels like this has been going on for years. Maybe Renee's right. Maybe everything is an illusion. It doesn't seem possible that any of this is actually happening.

The familiar pulse of conscious life trickles through the forest, calling me toward Amanda and Farren and Mom.

Stratton stops hard and reaches out his arm to keep me from moving. He tilts his head and narrows his eyes. I follow his gaze and hear the rustling of dry leaves and twigs snapping just up ahead of us. We duck down behind a fallen tree and steady our rifles, aiming the guns at whoever's out there.

From behind a cluster of spiraling thickets, two men and one woman emerge, heading toward our people. They carry assault rifles and don the tactical Southern Alliance outfits. They move cautiously and calculated.

I grab Stratton's forearm. "We can't let them reach our people."

He glances down at my hand on his arm and then quickly shifts to meet my eyes. "Okay, okay, I guess it's my turn to play."

As if my awareness has a mind of its own, my ability scans over the fighters and one of them feels connected to me. He's implant free.

I quickly pull my hand back. "Um, okay, but just go easy on them."

"I'm gonna do what I have to," Stratton says gravely.

Only a second or two passes and the implant free man stops cold in his tracks. The other two fighters loop around and question what he's doing. The manipulated man doesn't move or acknowledge them. I flit my attention to Stratton. He clenches his jaw, immersed in his Push.

"Jack, let's move," the woman demands. "What the hell you doing?"

The non-Influenced fighter quickly raises his weapon at the frozen man. "He's being influenced. Should I take him down?" His voice shakes with uncertainty.

"Hold on, man," the gruff woman barks. "It's Jack. We're not going to just blast him!"

Nervous energy prickles my skin and flows through my body. Every instinct inside tells me to turn away, but I don't.

Just as the man lowers his weapon, the manipulated man raises his pistol and fires on the woman, splattering blood on the other man's face before she crumples to the ground. The Influenced man looks indifferent to the situation, almost catatonic.

The second man raises his weapon, blood dripping into his eyes, but just as he does, the other man redirects his pistol at him. Two rapid pops rattle off and both men are dropped to the ground, motionless. This was a dual they both lost.

I cover my mouth in terror, somehow still not used to such violence. A heaviness sets in my chest.

"Hey, you alright?" Stratton asks, eyes wide with concern. "I'm sorry. I should've told you to turn away."

I force down the fear that's lodged in my throat and shake my head, hoping to erase what I just watched. No such luck.

"Was that necessary?" I ask, dreading the answer.

Stratton clears his throat. "It doesn't work that way for me. I'm sorry. I don't have the control that you do. We're not all as *special* as you." He turns away from me, lowering his head.

I grab his arm and lean forward. "Hey, I'm sorry, I didn't mean it like that. I...um...know that what your ability can do to others is hard on you. I've done my fair share of hurting people. We all have blood on our hands."

His face softens a bit as he glances at me. "I know I act like what I do is fun, but it's just a wall I put up."

I swing my weapon over my shoulder and place my free hand on his chest and look up at him. "You don't have to put a wall up around me. We are Influencers. I've got your back."

Stratton's chest rises and falls underneath my palm. He lets his weapon hang from the strap on his shoulder and slowly moves his hand over the top of mine. He gently squeezes my fingers. Our eyes meet and a wash of warmth passes through me.

I blink to regain my composure and yank my hand from his chest. Swallowing hard, I place both my hands on my weapon, redirecting it in front of me as I reposition myself a comfortable distance from him.

"Um...okay, we better keep moving." Stratton also readjusts his weapon, checking the ammo unnecessarily. "What are we going to do when we see the others?"

My breathing becomes short with each inhale. I'm not sure if it's because my mother, Amanda, Farren, and the others are up there or if something I shouldn't be thinking about is invading my mind. I force in a deep breath to steady my emotions.

As I release the air, I take a few steps forward and look over my shoulder at Stratton. "If Renee wants my abilities, she's going to get them. I'm going to throw everything I've got at her."

Stratton doesn't say a word and follows me. We navigate the tricky terrain and reach a steep drop-off. Looking over the edge, we see our people huddled together. Everyone with a gun is propped up on the perimeter of this gully they've holed up in. With the sun setting behind us, it's hard to make out who's who. Neither of our rifles have scopes and even if they did the darkness would make them useless. I have no choice but to wade into the unknowns of my awareness, fully aware there's a deadly shark is waiting for me there.

"Please don't leave my side," I beg to Stratton. "I'm going in."

Stratton takes a knee next to me. "I'll be your tether. I'm not going anywhere."

I draw in a deep breath and close my eyes, releasing the air slowly through my pursed lips. In the cover of darkness, I become more focused. It's like a blanket of security that conceals me from all the danger outside of my little bubble. Knowing Stratton is by my side makes entering the conscious awareness a bit easier as I slip into the great unknown.

The landscape of hazy shadows and rippling awareness expands before my mind. Below my mind's location, the assortment of ripples intersects into a vibrating display of enlightened consciousness, making it harder to find my beacon, Amanda.

My attention drifts in and out as I subconsciously prowl my surroundings for Renee's intrusive presence. My desire to free my people from her manipulative grip realigns my focus.

A sudden flutter consumes my heart as Amanda's powerful awareness reveals itself amongst the blur of people milling about below this ridge. I dial in on her and slip into her being, like stepping into a warm pool of flowing water. Blending with her consciousness, I access her recent memories. A vast projection of recent experiences explode before my mind. Overwhelming at first, I dissolve away all the recent mundane moments of the last few hours.

Flipping through her memories, I stumble upon one where Renee is addressing the group. I absorb the moment in time, allowing me to relive the memory from Amanda's personal perspective.

The vision starts with Amanda who pans over the group. Everyone is eagerly awaiting for Renee to speak as they sit in a half-circle in a small clearing between the trees. Amanda's unable to do anything other than sit and look straight ahead now. Renee paces before the gathering, her arms arrogantly folded across her chest.

"You are all the children of the new world that we will create," Renee boasts. "A world free of the human cruelty and primitive actions of your ancestors. Influencer power emerged for a reason." She stops a few feet in front of Amanda. "My plan is simple. I'm going to link all humanity to the greater awareness. Once they are connected, they will no longer be able to fall back on their destructive ways."

"You have no right," my mom snarls from where she sits on a stump at the far end of the group. "You are not a god. Non-Influencers have the same rights as any of us do. They have free will."

Renee takes in a deep breath and slowly pivots to face her. "Do we really need to go over this again? Just do your part, stay quiet, and I will leave your daughter alone as you demanded. Don't test my patience, please."

My mom's shoulders slump as she remains quiet. Renee glares at her for a moment before turning back to the group. Renee is about to say something when she furrows her brow and tilts her head toward Amanda.

She purses her lips before a grin lifts up on the corner of her mouth. "Hi Kaylin, nice of you to join us. But you're not welcome in this memory."

A white-hot light expands, fading out the vision. Heat floods over my shoulders and down into my fingertips, forcing me out of my Push. I gasp for air as I burst back into reality.

Stratton crouches down to meet my eyes. "Are you alright? What happened?"

I drop my hands to the ground to prevent myself from falling back as my jaw drops open. "It was... it was her.

She somehow kicked me out of a…a memory. How…I mean…what the hell is she?"

CHAPTER SIXTEEN

"I was watching one of Amanda's recent memories, and Renee somehow knew I was there." I shake my head, trying to rattle free the eerie feeling. "I don't even understand half of the things she can do. How are we supposed to stop her?"

Stratton nibbles on his lower lip. "I think you are a threat to her. It was you that freed her…"

I scoff. "Thanks for reminding me."

"No, no, no, that's not what I meant," Stratton insists. "I just mean, your ability is more powerful than any of us even thought." He stares up to the dark skies above. "If you can free her, you should be able to send her back too. Right? Or is that stupid?"

I jerk my head back slightly, pondering his words. *Is that possible? Do I have something inside me that I've not tapped into?*

I comb back the sweaty strands of hair that dangle in front of my face. "I mean, maybe. I don't know. All I know is that she's planning something pretty messed up. It sounds like she plans on locking everyone into some kind of personal subconscious network of hers. It's like she's going to hack into humanity."

"Well, we better act fast," Stratton urges. "If she saw you in that memory, she knows we're close."

My mind races back and forth with the endless ways this can go wrong. If we go in with our Push abilities blazing, we might get everyone killed. There has to be a way to weaken Renee without getting anyone hurt. Only one idea flickers into my mind.

I rise to my feet and Stratton joins me. "I'm going to go into my Push and get them all back. It's time to fight fire with fire."

Stratton pulls his rifle in tight. "Alright then, let's do this, princess. What do you need me to do?"

I pause for a moment, staring off into the darkened forest. "I'm going to hit each one of them one by one. As soon as I break them free from her influence, you need to use your ability and make them run however you can."

Stratton's eyes widen. He angles his head at me. "Okay, but you know what that means, right?"

Nodding slowly, I meet his eyes. "Just stop them before they do anything stupid. I just need them out of harm's way. Release them from your Push as soon as possible."

We gather our packs and weapons and tuck ourselves between a few large rocks and some thick hemlock tree trunks. As soon as we dive into our awareness, we will be both exposed, and there'll be no one that can protect our real-world selves. But there's no other way. I can't free them and manipulate them at the same time. It's just too much to focus on at once.

As if our bodies are a shield, we sit back to back on the damp ground in the small space. I quickly slip into my mind and force my consciousness on to the greater surroundings. My breathing slows and my nerves wash away.

The details of the darkened forest from our current reality dissolve and the familiar haze and diffused grey background floods my awareness. I pinpoint Amanda's overflowing awareness and quickly dive into her being. A flood of warmth and love explode all around me. I latch onto every emotion and feeling from her pure essence. I consume every bit of her and just like that, she is mine. Her awareness is free of any outside influence besides my Push.

Like Stratton and I planned, I release her just as soon as I connect with her. As my awareness pulls from her conscious spirit, I watch a subtle change in her conscious ripple. There's a break in the vibration for just a slight moment. And I know what that is. It's Stratton's influence.

Just as quickly as that change happens, I feel the familiar darkness that consumed my every being at the Magnus Order hub. Amanda is Stratton's now.

My love for Amanda makes me linger a moment too long, but I quickly refocus and begin searching for the next person to free. One by one, I liberate the non-implanted members of our group. With every person I free, a sense of dread follows. So far, I haven't felt Renee. There's a small chance she's not aware of what we are doing. More likely, she knows exactly what's going on and is waiting for the perfect opportunity to consume every part of my awareness. I'm worth more to her than all of them for reasons I don't understand.

Caiden is the last implant-free member of our group to be broken from Renee's spell. I release his awareness just as a familiar voice echoes in my mind. *"I'm not sure how, but you avoided my awareness."* The voice is almost muffled, but it is most definitely Renee. *"Unfortunately for you, I am much more connected to the conscious realm than you."*

Expanding my mind, I try to create distance from her ominous presence, but no matter where I try to hide her voice follows. *"It is such a shame you will not join me in making this world a better place. Even your friends know what I'm doing is right. Why fight it so hard? I'm giving you one more chance to be a part of this."*

"Get out of my head," I demand. "I won't let you do this. You're delusional."

A cool sensation washes over my awareness. *"I figured you would say this. It's a shame when we can do so much good with our abilities."* She goes silent for a moment before returning. *"I want you to know I truly did not want this for you. But you left me no choice. A person's past will always catch up to them."*

The coldness dissipates, and the hollowness of Renee's presence is filled by my greater awareness, warm and constant. She's gone.

Quickly, I evaluate the greater surroundings in this subconscious plane and realize there is no longer a connection to my people. A heavy sense of dread overwhelms me. I need to get back to reality... and quick.

Focusing on my real-world breathing, I'm able to reconnect with my body in the physical reality. Renee did not lock me in. I slowly open my eyes. I blink away the blurriness, taking a deep breath just as two strong hands grip my shoulders and yank me off the ground.

Pulling my head back, I meet the dark eyes of Billy Wilson. My chest tightens up in terror. Before I can react, Billy tosses me several feet in the air, and I slam hard on the forest floor, skidding several feet back into a large boulder. A sharp sting floods my back as I grimace in pain.

Billy slowly struts up and towers over me, his hulking shoulders rising and fall with adrenaline-induced rage. His eyes are lifeless, filled with an intense anger that I can only assume Renee is responsible for. She must've sent him. There's no way he would have found us on his own. But how did she get him here so quickly?

I flit my attention to where Stratton and I performed our Pushes and notice Stratton's legs emerging from behind the boulder. He's not moving. My breathing stammers as my heart squeezes into my throat.

"I can finally stomp you out, freak," Billy snarls as he takes a slow step toward me. "You should have never existed. And I'm going to rectify that now."

I try to push my body up, but the intense pain in my back spreads to my arms as they buckle. Billy hovers over me now as the half-moon dimly brightens the side of his face and the sweat trickling down over his scars. He hunches over and thrusts his arms forward, his hands clutching my neck. My eyes go wide as I can no longer breathe. I claw at his forearms, but his grip is relentless.

Gasping for air, I desperately concentrate on my Push, but there's no way I can focus. I try to kick him off but Billy pins down my legs with his heavy body. My chest seizes as my lungs beg for oxygen. White, flickering embers of light dance before my vision. The strength in my fingers and arms fade as I lose the ability to fight back.

I drop my arms down, accepting my fate. This whole day has been a terrible mistake. How could it have ended any other way? At least maybe some of my friends escaped...

Billy jolts back, eyes almost immediately glassing over. His mouth drops open and blood trickles out and down his chin. His meaty hands loosen from around my neck, and the air rushes back into my lungs as I suck in as much oxygen as I can.

Billy's arms go limp at his side as he slowly topples over to the forest floor. His falling body reveals Amanda standing over us with a bloodied knife in her hand. Shock fills her face.

Amanda tosses the knife and drops down next to me, gathering me up in her arms. "Kaylin, are you all right?" She looks over my body, searching for injuries.

I cough several times, trying to relax my throat. Looking up at her, a subtle smile inches up on my lips. "I'm ok...I think."

I shift my attention to Billy's lifeless body as my chest tightens. I was seconds from death.

Stratton!

"Check if he's okay," I beg, pointing at his limp legs lying several feet away.

Amanda nods and quickly stands. She carefully sidesteps Billy's body and makes her way over to Stratton. She leans down to check for a pulse, and after a few seconds, cranes her neck to look back at me, hope filling her expression. "He's alive."

An immense weight lifts from my shoulders as I take in a deep breath and lean back.

Dull pain in my lower back is all that remains from Billy's vicious attack. A wave of relief pours over me as I cautiously come to my feet. I race over and wedge myself between Stratton and the boulders we used for coverage. Reaching down, I gently stroke the side of his face as I notice a bloody bump on his head. Billy must've knocked him out first before trying to kill me. If we didn't take their weapons, he would have shot us both dead the minute he saw us.

A subtle groan escapes Stratton's lips as he comes to. His eyes flutter open and meet my gaze. He reaches his arm out, and I help him sit up. A grimace overtakes his face as he reaches back and touches his wound. "Ow, what the hell?"

"It was Billy Wilson," I say, looking over my shoulder at his dead body. "Renee sent him right at us."

He squints and finds Billy's lifeless body behind me. Quickly, he recognizes Amanda crouching next to me and narrows his eyes at her. "Amanda? How did you get here?"

Amanda pulls her long locks over her shoulder, playing with the frayed ends. "Well, after I woke up from my dark little experience... *thanks* for that by the way... I knew you guys had to be close." She looks over at me. "I know how Kaylin thinks. I searched for the highest point and just took off."

Anxious energy coils itself through my body. Planting my hands on my hips, I pace back and forth in front of Amanda and Stratton. "How many people did you free? Please don't tell me they're still affected by your Push."

"Relax princess," Stratton says as he slowly slides his back up the tree trunk to stand. "I got everyone who's implant free out of there. I diffused my Push right before I was knocked out."

I pull back my sweaty hair in a ponytail. Taking a heavy breath, I release the air and settle my nerves.

Amanda comes to my side and takes my hand into hers. She pulls herself in close to me. "I spotted a few people running through the forest as I was making my way here. I knew there wasn't time to get them to follow me. But I think they got away from Renee."

I wrench away from her as the fear returns to my exhausted body, forcing me to shake. "What about Farren... and my mom? What about the other Influencers?"

Amanda's face softens. "I don't know. By the time I snapped out of Stratton's Push, I was deep in the woods, away from them."

Stratton strides up to us. "I don't think Renee cares about them. All she needs are the Influencers. No one else matters."

I try to swallow the massive lump that's formed in my throat. Farren and Miya are both collateral damage because of their implants. They're expendable. And my mom still thinks I'm safe as long as she does Renee's evil bidding.

I take a step back. "I need to get down there and save the rest of them."

Stratton shakes his head. "No, we just freed all these people and need to regroup with them. Then we need to come up with a plan to get everyone else."

"No, it'll be too late," I insist. "You guys need to go gather everyone else up. Get far away from here. I'm the only one that can deal with Renee."

"We don't need you going in there all savior-like," Stratton says, eyes flattening as he glares at me. "We have to do this together."

Amanda raises a firm hand in front of Stratton. "Simmer down. You obviously don't know Kay like I do. She's already made up her mind."

I smile and shake my head. "You're going to want to listen to her. She only gets more annoying the harder she tries."

"Hey!" Amanda snarls and then lifts one eyebrow as her face relaxes. "Well, yeah, that's true."

Stratton picks up his backpack and digs through it. "Okay, but if you're doing this, you're going to need all the help you can get." He pulls out three small metal cylinders and holds them out at me. "These are flash grenades. You're going to need a distraction, and these might be just what you need without blowing everybody up."

I hesitate for a moment, but then grab the grenades and stuff them in my pack on the ground next to me. Strapping my rifle across my back, I turn to Amanda and Stratton. "Good luck, guys...I'll see you on the other side."

CHAPTER SEVENTEEN

CLIMBING DOWN A steep ledge, my legs shake as I try to find the next foothold. I pause for a moment, sucking in the crisp cool air of the night. Looking down, I find twenty or so feet more of dark abyss to scale down. Stratton said this would be the quickest route to get down from the ridge, but he forgot to mention how steep and sketchy this descent would be.

After several minutes of nearly slipping and dying, I finally reach the solid ground below. My fingers sting with fatigue and several small scrapes line my palms. Sweat trickles down my forehead, turning into a cold sweat as the dropping nighttime breeze brushes across my face.

I readjust my pack and ready my weapon. Avoiding using my flashlight, I carefully trudge through the overgrown forest floor. Every twig I step on sends a wave of terror up my spine. I refuse to use my ability in any way. Even feeling for the nearby awareness could signal my approach to Renee. Although, in the back of my mind I'm pretty sure she already knows I'm coming.

As I slowly make my way through the woods, all I can think about is confronting my manipulated friends and family. Jax and Ava are not being Pushed, but will they really fight me if I have a chance to stop Renee? I know as soon as my mom sees me, she will stand with me, but what about Farren? Renee was able to bypass his implant and pit him against me. I can't hurt him. I won't.

A flickering light in the distance grabs my attention. The eerie, amber glow filters through the tree line ahead. It's their camp. My pulse thuds behind my ears as I inch closer. I pull out one of the flash grenades for my pocket and ready it in my hand while gripping my rifle tight in the other. Muffled voices echo from up ahead. I can't make out who it is or what they're saying, but there is definitely more than one.

Pushing through my fear, I approached a thick pine tree and plant my back against its rigid bark lining. Just around its massive trunk, is the small clearing I saw in my Push. Peeking around the edge, I spot Ava and Envee tending to the fire in the middle of the opening. I quickly draw my head back and shift to the other side of the tree trunk. From this side, I see my mother talking to Jax and Miya. Farren and Renee are nowhere in sight. My chest becomes tight as my breathing quickens.

Where are they?

I might be able to take advantage of Renee's absence if I can get my mother's attention. I need to separate her from the others somehow. Neither Jax, Ava, nor mom seem to be using their ability to scan the greater consciousness. They're all preoccupied.

I glance down at the flash grenade in my hand. If I do this, I could hurt my friends, but what choice do I have? The effects of the flash and pop will only temporarily affect them. This is not a normal explosive grenade. I glance at my rifle. A lump forms in my throat as I swallow the uncertainty down.

Please don't force me to use this.

I draw in a slow breath and hold it for several seconds before letting it out slowly. Creeping around the tree trunk, I take one more glance at the clearing, and that's when I see her. Renee struts on the far end of the opening, Farren at her side. My heart races at the sight of him. He's armed and matching her pace, step for step. His hollow eyes reflect the fire. That beautiful life that I'm used to is gone, replaced by an empty gaze of manipulated obedience.

Anger boils in my stomach, flooding my body with adrenaline. Mixed emotions race through my mind.

You're not going to hurt him. You're not going to hurt any of them. Just throw the flash grenade.

I tighten my backpack straps and set my rifle at my side. Raising the grenade, I use my free hand to release the trigger clip. Holding the pin in, I take one last breath and spin out from behind the tree. Guilt sets in my stomach as I toss the grenade toward Renee and Farren.

Dirt kicks up off the ground as it bounces and rolls toward them. Spinning on my heels, I retreat to behind the safety of my tree and shield my eyes. A loud bang, followed by an intense hissing, rips through the forest, forcing me to flinch and crouch down.

For a second, everything goes quiet.

And then the screaming starts.

But they're not screams of terror. This is the sound of people I love screaming in pain.

I go numb, uncertainty sucking the blood from my face. This is all wrong. It was only supposed to frighten them, maybe temporarily blind them.

I don't want to look, but I have no choice. Craning my neck around the tree, what I witness threatens to end me with grief and horror as surely as I've ended all of them.

Farren lays on the ground, not moving. His leg nearly torn from his body, blood turning the dirt into a crimson mud.

Ava screams uncontrollably, and after several sweeps of the camp, I find Envee face down in the dirt, also not moving.

A few feet from them, Jax and Miya crouch over my mom who is flat on her back, hand over her face.

Pockets of fire dance all around the camp. Smoke hovers above the tree branches. My stomach flips as I realize I didn't throw a flash grenade. It was an explosive.

I've killed them.

The guilt is so great I can't even let myself cry or scream. I drop my pack and rifle and run into the clearing toward my friends and family.

Sprinting out from the tree line, my foot catches a root, and I fall forward sliding on the hard dirt surface, skidding to a stop just inside the clearing. The wind is knocked from my lungs. Waves of warmth radiates from the pockets of fire that surround me. I grit my teeth as the pain overcomes the adrenaline.

I manage to pull myself to my knees when I see Renee slowly stride toward me. The fire appears to part as she struts over. A determined glare hardens her face. Shock from the explosion paralyzes me.

"Look what you've done, you selfish child," Renee says calmly.

She cranes her neck to look at Farren's motionless body before turning over to look at my mother writhing in pain on the ground. Her unfazed glare returns to me as she shakes her head in disappointment.

Renee walks up to me and puts a hand under my chin, lifting my head to meet her eyes. "This is all your fault. Your foolish pride is going to kill your family."

CHAPTER EIGHTEEN

I WANT TO run to Farren and to my mother, but I'm frozen in terror as I kneel before Renee.

"I do not revel in your misery," Renee says softly. "This is not how I wanted this to end."

Through a low layer of smoke, I watch Ava cradle a motionless Envee in her arms, tears flooding down her face. A suffocating lump forms in my throat as I crane my neck to see Jax and Miya tending to my mother. She's alive but appears to be badly hurt. Numb from the guilt, I peer over at Farren who hasn't moved since the explosion.

I should be running to Farren. Why am I not running to him and the others?

"There's a way to fix this," Renee says, sucking me back to the current moment. "Nothing is permanent with conscious reality... All that truly matters is our subconscious awareness."

My shoulders slump and my breathing becomes shallow. With no hope, I meet her gaze. "You can't control life or death. I'm not falling for that crap."

A smile inches up Renee's face and she plants her hands on her hips. "Well, look at you one step ahead of me." She leans down. "You're right. I can't affect mortality, but I can bend the individual reality of anyone I choose."

Swirling nausea roils in my stomach as I drop back and sit on my legs. I narrow my eyes on her. "Is this not real?"

"It is for them."

She turns to Ava and Envee, saying nothing more.

Uncertainty consumes my mind as I twist my body and drop my hands onto the ground. "Ava? AVA?" I shout. "Please look at me."

Nothing. It's as if she can't hear me. She's only a few yards from me, but my frantic calls are not reaching her. I jump to my feet and stumble toward my mother, but each unbalanced step I take pushes her further away from me. I try to call out to Jax who kneels next to her, but the words refuse to escape my throat.

Spinning on my heels, I frantically run over to Farren. I'm able to reach him, but as soon as I try to place my hand on his chest an invisible force throws my arm back. All I can do is watch him slowly begin to squirm in pain, unable to open his eyes to see me.

My heart pounds and my legs go numb.

The scene blurs, and I'm instantly drawn back and kneeling before a smug Renee again. This time, I'm unable to stand. Everything happening here appears to be a Push-induced illusion. Everyone I care for is trapped in an intricate production meant for me. A weight is lifted off my chest as I realize my friends are unharmed, but that same heaviness sets on my shoulders as I know they're trapped because of Renee's obsession with my ability.

"You can't do this," I cry out. "What do you want from me?"

Renee's face hardens. "There it is. Now we are getting somewhere."

"Was this all about me?" I plead. "What can I do that you can't?"

Noticing I can't keep my eyes off my friends and family, Renee waves her hand out and everything dissolves into blackness. The forest and my family are gone, and all that remains is Renee and myself in the familiar silent void.

Renee sits, but there's no physical chair supporting her body. She crosses her legs and rests back as she tilts her head. "Reality isn't reality. There's only our awareness, but there are elements beyond my understanding—beyond my reach. If it wasn't for you, I would've been stuck inside my own personal awareness forever."

She once more waves her hand, but this time I'm instantly placed in a sitting position in my own invisible chair across from her. It's an odd sensation to feel nothing touching my body as I sit comfortably. The void is empty of light, but somehow we are illuminated as we stare at each other.

Renee sits forward and rests her elbows on her thighs. "Every time you visit my awareness, I sample more of who you are and what you're capable of. You've only tapped into a fraction of your true ability. But the most important thing you have is something I do not possess."

"And what is that?"

"Empathy," she says plainly.

I roll my eyes. "And how does my empathy for others fit into your evil master plan?"

She furrows her brow and glares at me. I must have hit a nerve. Renee huffs and purses her lips. She sits back and says nothing.

"Sorry to disappoint you," I scoff and adjust myself in my *magical* throne of air.

Renee refocuses and releases the tension in her face. "Why do you think freeing this world of the worst elements of human behavior is a bad thing?"

"You know what, no. Why don't you answer my first question instead?" I demand. "What makes my empathy so important to you?"

Renee sighs and relaxes her shoulders. "Very well. Empathy is more than a simple human behavioral trait. It's the foundation for our collective consciousness—the glue. Without it, reality would be fractured. Without a shared awareness, I believe our beings would cease to accept this existence. This has played out before in small samples. Hitler and his Nazi party is one example of a lack of empathy nearly eliminating a portion of humanity. This is happening again with the fear and hate for our kind."

I fold my arms across my chest and straighten up. "Okay, I get that there is a greater collective consciousness that we seem to be able to tap into, but I don't see how just because I'm empathetic toward other people, that it somehow makes me special."

Renee matches my posture and sits up. "When I first encountered you inside our shared awareness, an explosion of connections became accessible to me." Her gaze drifts off before she returns her deep brown eyes on to me. "I...I was lost and broken from the intertwined nature of the greater consciousness. When I was able to return to this reality, I realized how it was possible. Your ability goes beyond how you can affect others. You seem to be able to faintly fuse with every person you come into contact with. It's like you're creating neural pathways throughout humanity. And what's even more amazing is it seems your connection is like a cascading effect. Each person you come in contact with gives you access to every person that person came into contact with. It's like a daisy chain of awareness."

A coolness washes over my chest and settles at my core. I understand how she wants to use me now.

"I'm not going to do it," I snarl. "I'm not going to be your access point to inject your little virus into the planet."

That familiar smirk returns to her lips. "Oh, my dear, I believe you will. Your friends and family will not be able to last forever inside the nightmare I placed them in."

My mind flashes to Farren bleeding out, alone. Just as quickly as that memory fades, Ava losing Envee creeps in, and then there's my mother grasping at her burned-out eyes. The coolness in my chest fades and is replaced with the weight of a boulder, crushing me.

My breathing quickens as I frantically look into the void of darkness she's placed us in. I want to stand and run from her and try to get back to my family, but my body refuses to move.

"There's no use, honey," she says softly as she extends her hands outward. "You have your special talents, and I have mine."

I temper my breathing to steady my nerves. I inhale slowly through my nose and gently exhale through gritted teeth. Glaring at her, a helpless rage simmers inside me, unable to be unleashed. There has to be a way to get my family back without neutering humanity.

"What's the ultimate goal here? How does it end for everyone?"

Renee sits back while interlocking her fingers. She places her hands on her chin as she ponders my questions. "I told you. I want to end the cruelty that infects humanity. I will strip their primal rage from them. No longer will they seek conflict. I will give their lives meaning. They'll become what they're meant to be... an inferior branch of humanity that serves our kind as we transform this greater awareness."

I scoff. "You're no better than the power-hungry sector groups that used us to control their people."

"I was not around while these so-called sector groups infected the world. If I was, it would have never happened." She leans forward and drops her hands. "I've no intention of killing or harming any of the humans. I will not force them to do anything. I will simply strip them of their unevolved, primal tendencies."

"Lobotomizing them," I snap.

She lifts one brow. "Call it what you will. I see it far differently than you. I might even call it perpetual bliss."

I don't know why I'm arguing. I really have no choice, but to help her do what she wants. There's no way I'm going to let my friends and family suffer for eternity in the nightmare she's created. All the pain and suffering will drive them mad. That plus, I will never see them again. My throat locks as if Renee has her hands around my neck.

"So how does this all work?" I ask as my head drops in defeat. "What do I need to do?"

Renee's face brightens with joy, a deceitful smile spreading from ear-to-ear. "You don't understand the relief those words bring to me. Bringing pain onto fellow Influencers is something I never intended on. Most of all, I would never want to hurt the person that freed me from my conscious prison. I have a conscious connection with you that goes beyond human emotion. One day I hope you will feel the same way."

I shake my head. "Don't hold your breath. Just tell me what I need to do so you will set my friends free."

The empty darkness brightens and trees trickle into existence all around us. The chill from the crisp mountain breeze runs across my neck, sending shivers down my spine. The overwhelming floral and pine aromas attack my senses as if I've never smelled them before. We're brought back to the clearing where my friends and family remain in their manipulated awareness.

I jump to my feet and run to Farren. His leg is intact, and the blood has vanished, but he is still unconscious. The illusion Renee presented to me is gone. I quickly move over to my mother. She remains in the same spot on the ground but is no longer covering her face with her hands. I drop to my knees and grasp her limp hand. There's no sign of any injury. Jax and Miya lay comfortably at her side in their subconscious comas. Looking over my shoulder, Ava and Envee lay next to one another on a bed of decaying leaves. In spite of their apparent serenity, I know that mentally they are still trapped in Renee's illusion of pain and sorrow.

"Don't bother," Renee says softly. "My ability to alter reality around people is unbreakable. You've witnessed my void several times now. There's no escape. Are you ready to understand your place in all of this?"

I rake back several loose strands of my hair with my fingers and look up to the night sky. Stars flicker across an endless black canvas. The reality of what's about to happen sinks in. My stomach flutters as nausea roils. I take in a deep breath and hold it for as long as I can before I release it through gritted teeth. "Let's do this already."

Renee walks over to me and extends a hand out. "Let's begin."

CHAPTER NINETEEN

I can save them. I can save everyone.

I'm torn in two as I struggle with what's about to happen. Saving my friends and family only to doom the rest of humanity is a pretty heavy weight tied to my ankle.

"I've cleared the forest," Renee says calmly. "They'll be no interruptions. Please sit over here with me." She gestures to a moss-covered log at the edge of the clearing.

With every step, the pit in my stomach grows larger and larger, consuming my mind. As I walk, I glance at my family laying in the dirt, unaware I'm even here. A sense of dread washes over me as I realize there's a dark energy seeping out from them. I can feel their fear and sadness from the nightmare Renee's put them in. It's like an invisible fog that lingers all over my body.

And how much forest did she clear? What's become of Stratton and Amanda and the rest? And will she make me neuter my non-Influencer friends along with all the other humans on the planet? Could I do that to Caiden and

Erin and everyone else just to keep the people I love most alive? It seems like Jax and Ava will be on my side, but what will my mother think when she wakes up and I've sold my soul to this devil?

Stopping several feet before the fallen tree trunk, I stand motionless as I watch her sit down and eagerly wait for me.

"Come on now," she insists, her eyes narrowing on me. "This will not take long and then you'll have your family back."

All I want to do is run, but I sit down next to her. My shoulders slump and I lay my hands in my lap. "How is this going to work?"

Renee reaches out and grabs my wrist. I pull back a bit, but she does not let go. I swallow hard as she leans forward to make eye contact. "It's very simple. You're going to enter your awareness and I'm going to follow you in. I'm going to help you push further than you ever have before." She strokes the back of my hand with her thumb and chills rush up my arm. "Like an ocean, your awareness acts like water and touches everything as one enormous entity. You're the vast sea that binds humanity. Once we are in, I will have access to all the pathways that connect our greater consciousness. From there, the rest is up to me."

I want nothing more than to slam my fist into the side of her face, but our Push ability doesn't work like that. I know that would leave the others trapped in their private hell. Only she can free my family.

"If I'm going to do this, you have to promise that you will not connect to any of my people. Even the non-Influencers." I lock eyes with her. "You will not control any of them."

Her overconfident smile returns. "Of course, my dear. I'm not your enemy. Once this is done, you will come to realize this as well. Now, please open your full awareness to me and I'll do the rest."

Renee uncomfortably scoots closer to me on the log. She nods and says nothing more. My lips quiver and I bite down to stem the overflowing emotion.

I take one last look at my friends and release a fragile sigh before I close my eyes. A coolness races up my spine as my body relaxes. The conscious plane explodes before my mind as I fully immerse myself into my awareness. A heavy draw tugs at the back of my mind. Renee is linked with me.

The hazy horizon expands rapidly beyond anything I've experienced before. Shadows of connection dot the subconscious landscape as more and more people enter my reach. A surge of electricity pulses through my physical body and heightens my focus. My thoughts wander for a moment as I realize every new entity that manifests is another helpless soul that Renee we'll have access to.

My inner mind expands faster and faster as chains of connection spider out in every direction. Every person I connect to has countless pathways branching out from their awareness. It's as if I am water flowing down a hill and spilling out through endless channels as I expand further. The conscious bindings between everyone are endless as human interaction has bound us all. This can't happen. I can't sacrifice the world to save the ones I love.

I dig my heels into the conscious layers that tether me to this endless plane. The sprawling growth trickles as my reach retracts.

"What are you doing, my dear?" Renee's inner voice booms. *"This only ends one way for you and your friends."*

"I won't let you do this." My voice echoes throughout our shared awareness. *"I'm stopping this."*

"No, you are not."

A piercing screech vibrates through my inner mind. My physical body tenses as sharp pain flows from every limb. I try to pull myself out of my awareness, but it's useless. Renee has once more locked me inside.

The high-pitched sound softens just a bit as flashes of images pour out before me. I'm shown the nightmares my mother and everyone I love is trapped in. The terror and pain pour into my mind as if I'm living all of it at once. I want to scream but the pain in my mind and body refuses to relent, locking me in this terrible moment of total silence.

"Let go and let's finish this," Renee demands. *"You've only felt a fraction of what I can do."*

I'm about ready to give up when a soft voice whispers behind my ear. *"We are here. I love you. You're not alone."*

A warmth fills my chest. It's my mother. She's somehow managed to reach me.

Hearing her voice helps me realize that inside this shared awareness, I am connected to them. And not just them—Renee too. The empathy that binds me to everyone also entangles Renee's awareness. I was the one who pulled her from the abyss, and I can send her back.

Renee's constant attack on my senses burns behind my mind, but I push past that and find a quiet space tucked away deep in my awareness. The broadcasted terror from my friends and family fades into the background and all goes silent. Renee's intimidation tactics can no longer reach me. I have broken from her tether and once again control my awareness.

"*I knew you could do it.*" My mother's soft voice enters my sanctuary. "*You can stop her for good.*"

My perception spins in place desperately searching for my mother, but all that remains is the grey and hazy conscious landscape I've created for myself.

"*Where are you, Mom?*"

"*She still has my conscious awareness,*" her voice softens to a breathy whisper. "*There's not much time left. She's searching for you, and I don't know how much longer I can communicate.*"

The soft gray landscape darkens as unfocused rolling clouds spread across the horizon. A heaviness sets in my soul as I realize I'm running out of time. Renee's going to find me.

"*How do I stop her?*" I plead as dread closes in. "*Please. I can't do this alone.*"

"*You have to do this,*" my mother says as her voice cuts in and out. "*I believe in you. Push your awareness beyond anything you've ever reached. Consume her with your light and lock her inside again. Save us... Save everyone."*

My sanctuary begins to retract and collapse onto me. The swirling clouds of haze and conscious bindings become thick and dark as everything falls inward. Renee's close to finding me again. I'm running out of time. It's now or never.

I search inside my mind, hunting for that pure awareness that flows through every part of me. My focus allows me to disconnect from the crumbling conscious reality that's around my mind. I pull deep inside my awareness and connect with my Push ability. I refuse to hold back anymore.

Drawing everything I have inside, I force out my Push and it explodes from me, tearing away the conscious surroundings. The dark horizon ripples and cracks apart. Vibrant white light streams in from all angles as the subconscious plane turns into pure awareness. I push out farther and farther, as I draw in as many conscious connections as possible. I will overwhelm and smother Renee's awareness, locking her inside once more.

At the edge of my reach, I feel Renee's puny awareness, dwarfed by the vast connection I have formed. I lock in on her essence and try to smother her with the pure weight of my Push ability.

Renee's light flickers and I bear down, determined to end this.

Everything goes black.

My extended awareness is sucked out and I'm left feeling hollow. Mentally exhausted, I collapse into the darkness and float on my back, drifting in the emptiness.

"Mom, did I do it? Are you there?"

There's nothing until a dim point of light set far against the horizon shimmers through the darkness. My stomach flutters as hope returns. The white speck expands brighter and brighter, resembling a white sunset against a pitch-black sky. *"Mom? Jax? Farren? Are you there?"*

"Sorry to disappoint, but it is not them," Renee's inner voice echoes throughout the subconscious plane.

"No, it can't be," I plead as I force my essence to stand tall before the brightness. *"You can't be here. It's not possible."*

"Oh, anything is possible. You should know this by now. You are just a piece of this existence like everyone else. I only presented you with what you needed for motivation." Her voice draws into the center of the bright white sun. *"I truly wish you would have been by my side the entire time, but in the end, you did exactly what I needed you to do. You opened your awareness and gave me access to humanity."*

This can't be. A wash of hopelessness consumes my awareness, pulling my spirit down. I gave her everything she needed.

"Please, just let my friends go. Release them from the nightmare you have trapped them in."

The white orb flickers just a bit. *"They were never part of this. They never suffered for a second. This was all for you. I will always keep my promises. Your friends and family will not be connected to humanity's new future. They're free as long as they stay out of my way."*

My real-world body shudders as shock pours into every limb. My thoughts bounce back and forth between what Renee has done and how my friends and family are safe somewhere in the real world. My emotions are torn between relief and dread.

"Did I ever have a choice?" I ask.

"Every spirit has a choice. You chose to do what I presented before you." She goes quiet for a moment before her awareness once again swirls before me. *"I thank you."*

An echo from my real-world body flutters back to me, and I feel the tears streaming down my cheeks—the moistness trickling down like a waterfall.

"Just let me out of here. I want to go to my family."

The swirling white orb begins to pull back and lifts into the dark horizon. *"I'm afraid that's not part of the deal. I told you your friends and family would not be part of this. But I cannot have you interfering with the greater evolution of humanity. You will remain here, a shadow inside consciousness."*

"No! Please don't do this," I demand.

Pulsating waves dance on the bright orb as her presence dims. Seconds later, the bright light is gone and only loneliness and despair remain. I'm trapped inside the greater awareness.

I desperately try to extend my push and connect to anyone—anything, but as soon as I do the pitch-black surrounding dissolves into the gray and hazy forested backdrop. I feel no one and my ability is useless.

Desperate, I begin running throughout this conscious reality. I reach the hazy tree line and that's what I see them.

Diffused shadows stand motionless as far as I can see. An endless dark forest of ominous shadows extends for as far as my mind can project. I feel nothing from them. The once-great light of humanity is nothing more than a lifeless shadow now.

I am a ghost drifting between a graveyard of empty souls.

End of Book Three

***

Continue the Influence series:

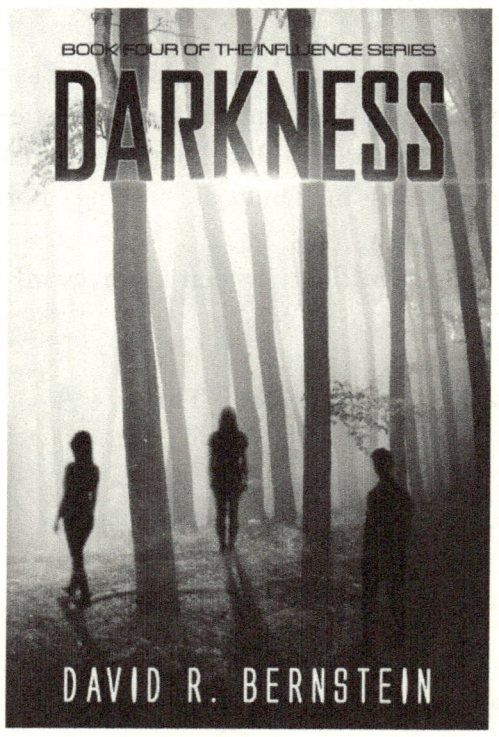

Free Origin Novella: Get 'Humanity's Protectors' (Influence Series Origin Novella) for free, giveaway opportunities, and other exclusive bonuses by joining my VIP List.

www.davidrbernstein.com

Thank you for reading book one of the Influence series. If you enjoyed reading this book, please remember to leave a review on Amazon. Positive reviews are the best way to thank an author for writing a book you loved. When a book has a lot of reviews, Amazon will show that book to more potential readers. The review does not have to be long—one or two sentences are just fine! I read all my reviews and appreciate each one of them!

www.davidrbernstein.com

Acknowledgements:
Special thanks to my wife, Brooke, for her support on this journey! I love you.
Thanks to all my family for the support!

Credits:
Chase Night - Editor
Jack Llartin - Editor
Torment Publishing

Made in the USA
Monee, IL
10 August 2020